ABOUT THIS BOOK

Escape to your favorite small town in the mountains, where spring has sprung and love and mystery are in the air.

When making a delivery for Shelf Indulgence, teenaged oracle Holly makes an unlikely friend with the town's recluse. Teeny Weeny Tahini's family continues to grow in a most surprising way. An unexpected guest crashes Willow Fairchild's baby shower. Visitors who wield the magic of the moon seek out help from town residents to recover their lost memories. The Howe witches and their new friends face a threat to the annual Flower Ball and Festival. Newcomer Judi inherited her aunt's cottage with its garden full of wonder—and killer plants. Addie Beaumont finds a distraction from heartache when the town's wards are breached and she and Michaela discover a dead body in the woods—but how did it get there?

These short stories, centered on the theme of fresh starts and new beginnings just in time for spring, are brought to you by *USA Today* and bestselling and award-winning authors in the Havenwood Falls Collective.

Authors in this anthology include:

- Belinda Boring
- T.V. Hahn
- E.J. Fechenda
- Morgan Wylie
- Kallie Ross
- Susan Burdorf
- Kristie Cook

DON'T MISS OUT!

Stay up to date at <u>www.HavenwoodFalls.com</u>

Subscribe to our reader group and receive free stories and more!

HAVENWOOD FALLS SPRING ANTHOLOGY 2022

HAVENWOOD FALLS COLLECTIVE

Published by

Ang'dora Productions, LLC

5621 Strand Blvd, Ste 210

Naples, FL 34110

Havenwood Falls and Ang'dora Productions and their associated logos are trademarks and/or registered trademarks of Ang'dora Productions, LLC

Cover design by Regina Wamba at MaeIDesign.com

INITIIS NOVIS

BELINDA BORING

CHAPTER 1

*T*he feel of the crisp March air stung at my nose, making each exhalation create a puff of white fog before my face. Where most of the country was enjoying the beginnings of the long winter thaw, Havenwood Falls was still knee deep in snow.

Literally.

I was sure my trek into the deep forest made my guardian, Micah, and his girlfriend Sedona, question my sanity, but there was a purity that came from hiking through the heavily laden trees while trying to catch a glimpse of the approaching spring.

The town was already abuzz with possibilities and what goals they had for the coming year.

New beginnings.

That seemed to be the current theme for most of the conversations back at Shelf Indulgence. Sedona was trying to talk Micah into redecorating our home, and when I left them both this morning, she had already started throwing new color scheme swatches at him, talking his ear off about how amazing it'll look and to just trust her.

They sounded like a married couple.

If I was a gambling girl, and I wasn't because *hello* . . . still a teenager, I'd say this could be the year that Micah finally stepped up and asked Sedona to be his forever.

That was one of the reasons why I'd announced I wanted to go see the falls and explore this morning over my pancakes and syrup. The logic behind it was if I wasn't around as a constant reminder that he couldn't fully let his guard down because of the *big bad* that we were hiding from, then maybe, just maybe, he'd soften his focus enough to see that the perfect woman was right in front of him.

True love didn't just happen in fairytales.

Sometimes you can find it in small, quirky towns in the Colorado mountains.

Anywho, I was determined to show Micah that we were safe, and other than my massive faux pas of using magic last Christmas and accidently turning him into a legit treetop angel, we could relax and attempt a normal life.

Well, as normal as a teenaged oracle and an angel in love with an empath witch could.

The snow crunching beneath my boots broke through my thoughts, reminding me that while I was all about helping love along, I was also indulging in my latest obsession.

Plants—more specifically magical plants that were in an abundance here in the mountains and around town.

Micah and Sedona had actually agreed with me when I made the argument that just because I couldn't perform magic right now, didn't mean that I shouldn't spend as much time as I could learning. Knowledge was as much a weapon as wielding the energy I felt flowing through my veins.

I was especially excited to explore the falls because unlike the rest of the area, the enchantment that pulsed in the aether there created a warm bubble of energy that felt stronger than anywhere else in town.

Magic acted different there—at least that's what I felt. Despite how cold the wind brushed against my skin now, turning the tips of my nose and ears pink, once I reached my destination, the warmth of the air would help defrost my freezing joints.

Just the thought of it made me speed up as I slid my gloved hands into my pockets. I'd come prepared, having learned my lesson the first winter we were here and almost getting frostbite. Today's attire consisted of my favorite long-sleeved fleeced sweater, jeans, heavy winter coat, two scarves, and a beanie. I snorted. Once I got to the falls, I'd be sweating because of all the layers.

Almost there. Just through this last stretch of pines and over the next crest, I thought as excitement bubbled within me.

Fallen branches cracked beneath my steps, pushed into the snow from my weight. Whether it was my imagination or not, my entire body seemed to thrum with magic. Goddess, I loved living here in Havenwood Falls. This was the first time in my entire life where I didn't feel like a freak amongst a sea of normal people. Energy was infused into the very fabric of the town. I no longer felt alone.

I shook my head, clearing it of the random thoughts that tumbled about in my mind. I was here for a reason . . . to see what kind of plants grew around the Falls and whether I was getting better at identifying them.

My goal was to eventually convince Micah to let me start my own interesting collection in a backyard garden. I'd already tested the waters with Sedona, knowing full well if I could get her on my side, she'd help plead my case.

I snorted out loud this time. My mind was all over the place this morning, reminding me of the squirrels that liked to scurry around the square looking for dropped food.

"Get it together, girl," I teased, knowing full well I was talking to myself. "You can worry about all that later. Just focus on the moment."

I took in a cold breath and readied myself for the onslaught of green that awaited me, when a sound filled the air—a beautiful, grief-filled voice singing.

The melody was coming from up ahead, and it stopped me dead in my tracks, demanding that I give it the attention it deserved. The haunting notes seemed to hang on the snow crystals that danced as they fell from the above trees. Emotions churned within me, making my heart hurt and weep for the person singing.

A man.

Micah had warned me that even though Havenwood Falls was the safest place we'd ever lived, I still had to remain vigilant and this, this was definitely something he'd expect me to be cautious about. It wasn't every day that I heard someone sing such a tragic tune . . . alone . . . deep in the woods . . . during winter.

Part of me knew this was one of those situations where I needed to carefully retreat and rush home, but there was no denying the pain the singer infused in each word.

There was something solemn in its nature, almost reverent in the way each note worshiped.

Peeking through the trees to maybe catch a glimpse before leaving, I let out a soft sigh as I caught the outline of a man crouching on the snow. He didn't appear dangerous. If anything, there was something that felt vulnerable about the stranger.

Realizing this wasn't a moment that required an audience, I slowly stepped backward, desperately trying not to make a sound.

I failed.

There was a soft swish of snow like the gentlest of whispers, yet he heard it.

Whipping up and about, he scanned the area, and like a deer caught in the headlights, our gazes met, freezing me to the spot.

He saw me. He must've known I'd heard him singing, violating his privacy.

My chest began to burn from the air caught in my lungs. I couldn't breathe, let alone will my body to move. I wanted to tell him I was sorry, that I hadn't meant to intrude, but that my curiosity had gotten the better of me.

Curiosity killed the cat, right?

All I could hope was he wasn't some serial killer a second away from severing my head from my shoulders.

"Shut up," I muttered low beneath my breath. "Stop thinking everyone's a threat."

The man bristled like he heard, which should've been impossible given I barely spoke louder than the wind whistling softly about me. That was one of the issues living in Havenwood Falls—I was also surrounded by those with inhuman senses.

"Crap." I closed my eyes for a second as I prepared myself to run. Gone was the magical melody that had kept me rooted to the spot. The coldness of the snow had now begun mingling with the fear that filled me.

He took a step toward me, raising his hand in front of him.

"Wait."

One word, but like the gullible fool I was proving to be, I paused.

CHAPTER 2

"*J*ust don't kill me," I joked, inwardly groaning at my ill-timed sense of humor. If I survived this, I was dangerously close to Micah doing it himself for being so reckless. I steadied my nerves, holding my hands to stop them from trembling. "I'm sorry."

The stranger took another step toward me.

"I'm not going to hurt you." And as if to prove he was speaking the truth, he moved to the side, revealing what he'd been focused on. "I give you my word."

A bazillion voices exploded in my head, most of them screaming for me to run. There was just one small thought that peeked through, reminding me of something Micah had told me about. One of the beautiful things about Havenwood Falls was that it was hard for strangers to go undetected within the town's magical wards, and that very little surprised those in charge of keeping the residents safe.

I might not have seen this man before, but that didn't mean he didn't live here.

"Why should I trust you?" I countered, my body still primed to flee.

He gestured to the ground beside me. "Last time I checked,

it was you who intruded on a private moment."

His lips curled into a sad smile, reminding me of the melody he'd been singing.

"I heard your voice," I answered honestly. He didn't feel dangerous, but that didn't mean anything to the fear that prickled my skin. "You seemed so sad."

At the mention of me overhearing him, grief flooded his features, causing me to come closer. There was some kind of innate need for me to help, to see if I could somehow ease his suffering. As I closed some of the distance between us, my gaze dropped to what he revealed by moving.

There at his feet was a small photo frame with a beautiful woman smiling tenderly out from it. That wasn't what piqued my interest all over again and had me walking toward him.

It looked like he was kneeling before some type of altar or memorial. Peeking up through the white, cold snow was the glowing stalks of a flower that pulsated with magic. That still wasn't exactly what enthralled me though.

With each step I took, the plant grew—breath for breath, glowing and twinkling with animated life.

"What is that?" I whispered, not wanting to do anything that might disrupt the scene before me. Part of me was scared if I blinked, the plant with disappear like an illusion, and I deeply hoped that it was real.

"*Initiis Novis*," the stranger answered in Latin. "It means new beginnings."

I was now right beside him, and together we watched as a miracle unfurled before us.

Along the green stalks of the glowing plant, I could see sparks of magic ignite and weave along the surface. With the kind of energy flowing from it, I expected to see puddles of water mixing with the soil to make mud, but it remained untouched.

As each second passed, an extraordinary scent filled my lungs. Small buds appeared before bursting into the most vibrant flowers of yellows, reds, and oranges. The colors were unlike anything I'd ever seen before—the depth and intensity seeming otherworldly.

There was no way this plant came from this world.

This was something created from pure, unadulterated magic.

"What is that?" I repeated, unable to find the right words to ask the questions I had, like where did he find this flower and why hadn't I ever seen in it in all the research I'd been doing? Now I was wishing Sedona and Micah *were* here just so they could help me find out its origin. Maybe the answers were located in the libraries up at the academy. I wondered if Micah would even let me go and find out.

My eyes never once left the now trembling, fully bloomed flower.

"Ssshh," the stranger said, holding his arm out to stop me from moving. "Wait."

Silence filled the air.

The ground shook ever so slightly beneath my feet, causing the petals and leaves to sway and shimmer right before everything went still—deathly still.

The stranger gasped, wetting his lips as he stepped forward and dropped to his knees. His hand reached forward, quivering with restraint. I could tell he wanted to touch the flower, but something held him back.

Fat tears fell from his eyes and rolled down his cheeks.

No matter how many times I replayed the next few seconds, I couldn't ever tell which came first—the explosion of energy or the one name he uttered with absolute love and devotion.

A burst of air rushed past me and where the glorious flower once grew, there now stood a woman . . . a ghostly woman.

She had long dark hair that was curled and pinned up into an elegant style. Her clothing wasn't modern—in fact, I'd say she was possibly from the nineteenth century because of the ruffled petticoats I saw peeking out underneath her wide skirt. Her skin glowed, but that wasn't what my gaze fell on.

No, it was the way she looked with equal adoration at the stranger.

The way her lacy gloved hand stretched forward as if to pierce the veil and actually touch his whiskered jaw.

"My Catriona," he murmured. The emotion in his voice was thick enough that it caused a lump in my own throat to form. The last thing I'd expected to find when I left the house this morning was such an innocent display of devotion.

"My darling Marcus," the ghostly woman replied.

My breath hitched as I watched them desperately want to embrace each other—their love almost palpable. They didn't utter any more words. Instead, they simply spoke volumes with their eyes until both sensed their time had run out.

The woman began to flicker, the spectral glow around her body beginning to fade. Panic filled her eyes and a mangled sound erupted from the stranger.

"Please," he begged, choking on his tears. "Just a few moments longer. It isn't enough."

I took a step backward. I shouldn't be here. I should've left when I first stumbled across him singing alone. If I'd thought he'd been vulnerable then, this was even more exposed.

Despite the crunching of the snow beneath my feet, he didn't once glance away from the woman he loved. He didn't seem to blink even as she slowly faded away into nothing but a whisper.

The wind held her last words—an utterance that broke my heart.

"Forever, Marcus. Forever."

As an agonized sob wrenched from his throat and he crumpled forward to where she once stood, I didn't stop to comfort him.

I couldn't.

I ran from his tears.

I ran from my own.

I ran from the magic laced with pain.

CHAPTER 3

*N*o matter how many ways I tried to word my searches, the Internet provided no answers. Add to the fact that I'd scoured almost every magical book I'd been able to lay my hands on, and I was coming up with a big fat nothing.

The glowing flower that turned into a ghost was still a mystery, and it bugged me to no end.

It wasn't that I was a glutton for punishment . . . well, I was, but I wasn't focusing on the sorrow that I still felt remembering Marcus and Catriona, the two strangers. I didn't enjoy reliving those moments between them or the helplessness that seemed to exude from them.

Love wasn't meant to hurt like that—to feel so all-consuming that death would be a welcome relief.

That wasn't what I thought each night when I lay in bed and the scene repeated over and over in my mind. No, that was the truth I saw embedded into their features with such clarity that I could almost taste their longing to be reunited.

Did a love like that truly exist, and if it did, which obviously it must because I saw it, should it really be classified as love? It felt cruel . . . unfair . . . unbelievably devastating to ever be paired with the emotion I saw between Micah and Sedona. I couldn't imagine them staring at the other with such desperation. I still struggled to find the right words to describe it.

All I knew was my heart still ached so I did the one thing I knew best—I focused on what I could control. I obsessed over the flower and finding out what kind of magic made it possible.

I'd spent the past week with burning questions on the tip of my tongue. I wanted to confide in Sedona what I'd seen and ask if she'd ever come across spellwork that could produce that kind of enchantment. Addie had even come into the store—someone I knew was a magical badass. If there was anyone in Havenwood Falls who would know or could find the information I was seeking it was her, but I choked when I'd seen her. By the time I'd found my courage, she was out the door and on her way.

Asking questions shouldn't feel like a betrayal to my promise to Micah to not dabble in power I didn't understand. It wasn't like I wanted to create my own flower and summon the monster who hunted me. I wasn't *that* stupid, even though for a microsecond the thought did tempt me.

No, I was going to stick to research and learning all I could. Which was why this afternoon I was going to see if Tempest and Natalie could sneak me up to the Academy to search through the libraries there. The mystery of the flower demanded I exhaust every possible avenue before I give up.

"Ugh," I exclaimed, pushing away from the makeshift desk Sedona had set up for me. The cute décor and knickknacks I'd collected to add personal touches annoyed me—like the obsidian carved cat and agate goldfish mocked me for not being smart enough.

"It can't be that bad," Sedona said as she popped her head around the bookshelves.

A new shipment had arrived, which meant she was rearranging displays and cataloging her growing inventory. Soon it would be time for her to update the windows for upcoming spring, and this year she wasn't telling anyone what the theme was yet. Knowing her, it wouldn't be something easy like bunny rabbits, flowers, and Easter eggs. Sedona had too much creative flair not to go all out.

I rubbed my face with my hands and let out a tired sigh. This would be where I'd probably take a break or a nap, but this newfound obsession wouldn't let me. Glancing over at the half-eaten egg salad sandwich that sat on the plate, a spear of pickle ignored beside it, I knew I'd at least need to finish lunch before diving back into reading.

I lifted the sandwich to my mouth, poised to take a bite. Sedona had even added pickled sliced beets, a personal favorite of mine, but that didn't even tempt me. I had zero hunger.

"Well, crap," she teased as she watched me place the sandwich back untouched. "I never thought I'd see the day that you'd turn your nose up at chilled beets." I knew she was studying me as if to gauge what was going on, and for the hundredth time that day, I just wanted to blurt out my questions and be done with it.

Once again, I said nothing. There was something so personal and private about what I'd seen that by talking about the flower with someone else, it felt like I was sullying the couple and what they shared. Maybe the answer laid not in discovering what the flower was, but in finding the stranger called Marcus and seeing whether he could tell me about it himself.

"There's a first for everything," I replied, trying to lighten the mood. If Sedona worried, then Micah would notice, which would then lead to him worrying. Once that ripple effect was set into motion, it was only a matter of time before it led him to me. So, instead of confiding in her, I decided to tease her right back. "Gotta keep you on your toes. Can't have you knowing all my secrets."

That was the wrong thing to say because instead of her laughing it off like I'd hoped, frown lines deepened on her brow.

Crap.

"You feeling okay?"

Double crap.

I lied through my teeth. "Of course. You know me. Once I find something that interests me, I become hyper-focused." I didn't flinch when her eyes squinted a little—like she could read my mind. Which she couldn't. She was trying to read my emotions. Thankfully I'd learned from the best when it came to protecting myself from other people's powers and gifts.

I simply stared at her, letting Sedona know I knew exactly what she was doing.

"Sorry." She actually looked like she was. "I'm just not used to you refusing food."

I rolled my eyes, reached for the sandwich, and took an exaggerated bite. The tang of the beets zinged against my tongue right before the creaminess of the cheese and crispness of the lettuce filled my mouth. Damn, this was a stellar sandwich.

"Satisfied?" I chewed deliberately, resisting the urge to open up and stick out my tongue before I swallowed. "I promise I'll have an extra helping of dinner tonight, okay?" It was my turn to study her.

Sedona nodded, and with that, the air lightened. When she worried, you could always feel it, her magic coming off her in waves.

Peering around me, she pointed to my desk. "What are you working on that has you so frustrated? Anything I can help you with?" She took a step toward the pile of books I had stacked to the side. Without thinking, I countered her, my body blocking her from reaching them.

Damn, if she wasn't worried about me now, she'd be suspicious. I was acting like I had something to hide.

I picked up the glass of iced cola that was leaving a wet circle of condensation on the desk and took a long sip. This gave me a chance to gather myself and hopefully show her I wasn't acting weird.

"I'm still trying to learn more about the plants around here. I have a hunch that because this is Havenwood Falls, the magical properties of herbs and flowers would be a little different." She eyed me closely. "Not that I'm wanting to do magic, I promise. I just want to learn." And with that declaration, I moved over so she could see for herself. Luckily, I didn't have the notes I'd written about the flower out in plain sight.

Her sigh of relief was audible.

"You thought I was cooking up some scheme to turn Micah into something else, didn't you? Perhaps a giant Easter bunny so you could use him in your window display." Just the thought made me giggle.

Sedona's eyes widened. "Don't even joke about it, Holly!" she exclaimed, hand covering her mouth. "Although . . . "

It was my turn to gasp. "You seriously pictured it, didn't you?"

Her cheeks flushed a bright pink as she tried to control her laughter. "With a pretty blue plaid bowtie to match his eyes!"

"To match what?"

I swear the man needed to wear a bell or something because Micah had an uncanny way of sneaking into conversations and scaring the crap out of me. The man didn't even make a sound when he moved—he had the stealth skills of a ninja.

"Micah!" I snorted, not knowing how much he'd heard. "How good are you at hopping?"

Sedona burst into laughter, her body shaking from the strength of it. "And how do you feel about carrots?"

Confusion flooded Micah's face, making our questions even funnier. He was completely oblivious. Thank goodness.

"I'd hate to interrupt you both, but I actually need to ask you a favor Holly." I could tell he was dying to ask us what was going on but bless the angel and his ability to focus.

"Tell me what it is so I can hop right to it."

The sound that came out of Sedona's mouth in response was hilarious. "Holly!"

Micah shot a curious glance at Sedona and then back at me. "Seriously, guys. Can we focus for a second? This is important."

He had a package wrapped in brown butcher paper, the same kind that we used when we delivered orders to people in town.

I instantly sobered. For a moment. "What's up, Doc?"

Sedona and I both howled, unable to breathe from laughing so hard. Tears streamed down my cheeks, and I knew this was mostly due to releasing the frustration I'd been feeling. By the time I finally stopped, and Sedona was hiccupping beside him, I felt more like myself than I had all week.

"You're a pair of weirdos." Micah shook his head at us, clearly the odd man out. "And while I wish I understood the joke, Professor Knox is waiting for this, Holly. I'd take it myself, but I'm needed back at the Academy for class. He should be there for the next hour so go to the address and give it to him."

The look he gave me stopped any further joking around, and I nodded. "Want me to text you when it's done?"

There was a good chance he wouldn't get my message because the mountains often messed with the wi-fi signal, but I always sent one anyway.

"Sure. Then come straight back." Micah peered over at my desk, no doubt seeing what Sedona had earlier—he was familiar with how I got with new projects. "The fresh air will do you some good, and when you return, help Sedona out in the store. Too much study isn't always a good thing. Give your brain a break." He pulled me in for a hug, planting a light kiss on the top of my head. "Love you."

He meant it, too.

"Love you more," I fired back, already heading to where my coat and winter gear was hanging. While the town wasn't as a snow packed as the mountain and forest, it was still super cold outside. "Love you too, Sedona!" I hollered.

The bell over the door tinkled as I opened it. That first hit of wintery air hit me hard. I pulled up my scarf, so it sat like a mask over my nose.

Maybe on the way back I'd stop by Coffee Haven and grab a

hot chai latte, the thought already sending a rush of warmth through me.

It would take about fifteen minutes to reach Professor Knox's home and then fifteen minutes back. Maybe, if I was lucky, I'd arrive at the coffee shop in time for a batch of gooey chocolate brownies fresh out of the oven.

Sounded like a great way to spend the rest of the afternoon.

CHAPTER 4

*H*oly. Smokes.

Despite knowing where the address Micah gave me was, it hadn't really hit me how far up Eighth Street it was or just how fancy the house would be. We'd known Knox for a while now, but this would be the first time I'd personally come here. Hell, if I'd known I'd be standing in front of a home I would only describe as palatial, I'd have dressed up a little.

I took pride in the clothes I wore, liking the style I'd developed over the years, but something told me if I wasn't careful, I'd probably scuff the fancy tile foyer with my cheap sneakers. I stared down at my feet, somewhat awkwardly. The Converse-like shoes looked amazing at the consignment store where I found them a few months ago.

Now, they just looked out of place.

"Who the heck is Professor Knox when he's not a teacher?" I muttered beneath my breath. I was the last person to judge a book by its cover, or in this case an owner by his house, but this mansion wasn't something a person bought on an academic salary.

Resisting the urge to turn around and tell Micah I'd gotten lost, I gathered all the courage I had and approached the front door. Well, the front gate because there was no way the occupants would allow visitors to just wander in off the streets.

I pressed the button on the intercom and bounced softly on my feet, trying to keep warm. Those brownies were sounding more and more delicious by the moment.

"Hello?" I recognized the professor's voice over the speaker.

"Hey, Mr. Knox. It's Holly. Micah sent me." I felt silly talking to the small electronic box attached to the wrought iron gate. Somewhere there was a camera pointed at me to make sure I was who I said I was.

"I see you. Let me buzz you in and come up to the front door." The intercom clicked off, and I heard a loud sound as the gears creaked to life and the gate slowly swung open.

I tried not to gawk as I walked through, peering around for the camera I knew was there. I could only imagine the professor laughing as I almost jumped out of my skin when the gate clanged closed. Rolling my eyes, I quietly chided myself for being so jumpy.

Even with all the snow that had kept Havenwood Falls buried over the past several months, the front yard still looked magical with the white flakes coating sculpted bushes. The closer I got to the house, however, the more I felt the tell-tale tingle of magic as the iciness gave way to lush greens and a beautiful tinkling fountain. If I wasn't already tracking in snowy footprints, I'd have assumed that it was mid-spring based on how fresh everything looked.

What the heck did Mr. Knox specialize in again? I wondered, racking my brain for the tidbits I'd heard from Micah. He'd lived in Havenwood Falls since just after its founding and had come over from England where he'd studied alchemy. Whenever I'd tried to listen closer, Micah had dropped his voice and spoke in hushed tones. There was mystery that surrounded the professor, but until now I hadn't really given it much notice.

There was nothing like approaching a person's home to spark the imagination and get the questions firing.

The front door was ajar, and as I hastily wiped my feet on the mat in front of me, I heard Knox welcome me in. "Don't be afraid, Holly. I'll be down in a moment. Come in and make yourself at home!"

His voice came from deep within his home—perhaps from upstairs based on the gorgeous curved staircase that greeted me in the foyer.

"Okay," I replied tentatively, worried that if I spoke too loudly it would echo throughout the house like the Grand Canyon. Tugging my gloves off with my teeth, I carefully stuffed them into my pocket. The last thing I wanted to do was traipse the cold outside over the immaculate flooring.

This place was exquisite, and honestly, a little more lavish than I thought the professor's tastes were. Not that I didn't think he had nice things, but this was a level of richness that I'd never seen before. A crystal chandelier hung above me, and it was hard not to become enthralled by the way the light reflected off each facet, casting rainbows across the walls. Beautiful flowers adorned the side tables in vases that looked old and vintage. The artwork was what drew me in, however. Whomever the artist was, there was such a boldness in each stroke of color—the landscapes and portraits whispering of stories that begged to be shared. The person had a gift.

Standing there in the foyer, it was hard not to feel small. Somewhere in one of the rooms I heard the faint ticking of a clock, a reminder that I had things to do and places to be.

"Professor Knox?" I called out with the hope he'd answer. Nothing. Wherever he was, he was out of ear range.

Another sound reached me—the crackling of a fireplace. The feeling in my fingers and toes still hadn't quite returned and remembering that he'd told me to make myself at home, I couldn't fight the need for warmth any longer.

It wasn't until I checked the third room that I found the source of temptation. The room looked like it was decorated straight out of the history books I'd studied from last year, which made sense considering when Professor Knox had arrived in town. I tried not to get hung up on the fact that considering how old he was, he looked about the same age as Micah. While he wasn't an angel, he must've found some sort of immortality or way to stay young.

Gently placing the package down on the nearest table, I wasted no time in standing before the fireplace, heating my hands first before turning about to warm the rest of me.

This room didn't have the museum feel of the other rooms I'd stolen a peek of. I spied the book that was left open to where someone had last read. An empty teacup sat on top of a matching saucer beside the book. Nerves flittered in my stomach. Had my arriving interrupted the professor or was there someone else here?

Again, I noticed the flowers, and with a smile curling of my lips, I left the warmth of the hearth to see if I could identify what kind of flora it was. They reminded me of roses but there was something a little different about the way the petals curled around each other, and the scent that filled my senses when I bent down to smell them. A rose, but not quite a rose.

Whatever they were, they were gorgeous, and if I was brave enough, I'd ask Professor Knox for one to take home.

Which brought me back to the elusive man. I was pretty sure I'd been here a good ten minutes, and he'd yet to make an appearance. Now that I was warm enough to venture back out into the snow, maybe I should just leave and head back to the bookshop—package delivered.

That's when she caught my eye.

The woman.

The ghost.

"Catriona?" I whispered, completely spooked. Hanging on the farthest wall was the portrait of the strange woman I'd seen by the falls a week ago. She had the identical dark hair that was curled and pinned into a soft bun on top of her head, and her eyes . . . there was no mistaking it was her. What surprised me even more was bundled in her arms was a tiny baby—her baby.

"Who are you?" I asked the portrait, knowing full well she couldn't answer as I approached. I could instantly tell that the same artist who'd painted the artwork in the foyer had also captured her likeness perfectly. She was stunning.

"What are you doing in here?" The question thundered through the air and caused me to jump in surprise. I hadn't heard anyone enter the room, and as I whipped about to apologize, I came face to face with him.

The stranger.

The man she'd called Marcus.

"Sir," I stammered, my mouth instantly dry with fear. He looked nothing like last week when he'd appeared vulnerable and sad. No, today, this man stared at me with such an intensity that I forgot how to form words. I kept gulping in air, hoping against hope that the professor would show up at the door and save me.

"Who said you could come into this room? Who were you talking to? What did you touch?" he demanded again, the veins in his neck starting to bulge with anger.

It was his room I'd entered—his book—his empty cup of tea.

I backed away from him, skirting about until I was closer to the door. He watched me like a hawk, standing his ground but letting me know that should I provoke him, he'd strike.

"I'm . . . I'm . . . I'm sorry!" I exclaimed and rushed for the door, crashing into Professor Knox as he reached for the door handle.

"Holly?" he replied, startled. "Are you . . . " He didn't bother finishing his sentence because as he followed my frantic glance back over to Marcus, he realized why I was trying to escape. He reached for me, hoping to calm me. "Give me a moment, Holly, and I'll explain. Please." He gently squeezed my arm before letting me go, his gaze now firmly on the man behind me.

I didn't wait for him to excuse me. I left and didn't stop

when I heard the door click shut. Raised voices came from within the room, but I'd learned my lesson about curiosity.

It killed the cat.

The end.

No one won by sticking around and overstaying their welcome like I just had.

Ignoring the way my sneakers squeaked over the foyer tile, I quickly closed the front door and ran to the iron gate, not realizing that I needed someone to open it.

"Damn it," I cussed, debating whether or not I should take my chances with climbing up and over it. I wasn't exactly the most graceful person on the planet, but I'd rather fall flat on my face than go back to the house and ask for help.

There was a loud click, and the gate swung open.

That was all the invitation I needed. I ran through and didn't stop until I barged into Shelf Indulgence, the bell clanging loudly.

"Holly?" Sedona asked, peering up from the front counter. "You okay? You get the parcel delivered?"

"Mm-hmmm." I nodded, my hands shaking. I plastered on a smile and gave the finest performance of my life. "You got something for me to do?"

She did, of course, and the rest of the afternoon was spent trying to desperately forget the look of fury in that man's eyes.

It wasn't the only thing that had slipped my mind.

I'd also forgotten the brownies.

CHAPTER 5

"*H*ow do you not weight a ton, Micah?" I groaned, pushing my now empty bowl away. While I'd barely been able to make it through the huge serving of homemade chili with fresh cornbread, he'd somehow managed to devour three entire bowls.

"What can I say?" He grinned, scooping up the last bit of sauce with his finger. "Angelic metabolism."

Sedona whacked him with her hand before I could. "It's not polite to brag, Micah," she scolded. "Some would even call it a sin."

Wiping his mouth on the napkin from his lap, he stood to begin gathering the dishes so he could take them into the kitchen. "It's not a sin if it's the truth, sweetheart." This time he was able to side swipe her attempt at hitting him. "But that temper of yours . . . " He tsked loudly. "That right there isn't a virtue, and you know it."

She was ready to get up and argue some more when there was a loud knock at the front door. She glanced at Micah—exchanging some secret message between them because a second later, he shook his head.

"You?" he asked.

She replied with her own silent refusal.

"Don't look at me," I fired, raising my hands in defense. "I'm the one with the least number of friends here. No one's going to be trekking through the snow at night just to come braid my hair and gossip." That confession used to kill me when I was younger, whenever I watched other kids my age goofing around together. I hated being different from everyone and always feeling like I was on the outside looking in.

Now I viewed it as my superpower—this way there was less teen angst and drama.

Micah had softened the blow by adding that it meant he only had to deal with mine so thank you. He had a point.

We stood there looking at each other as the person at the door continued to knock loudly.

"I think the polite thing to do would be to answer," I suggested with a hint of snark.

Micah shot me a warning glance before hurrying out of the dining room toward the front of the house. There was a slightly muffled greeting as he saw whoever was on our doorstep, followed by the sound of our visitor entering.

"Sedona. Holly. Want to join me in the living room for a moment?" There was no indication about who'd braved the cold, and my only assumption was it could one of two people—either Addie had come to talk to Sedona about Coven business, or it was someone from the Academy to talk with Micah. It wouldn't be Tempest or Natalie because they were considered family and knew not to knock.

Our casa was their casa.

Following behind Sedona, my heart thudded loudly in my chest when I heard Professor Knox's voice. He spoke in hushed tones so I couldn't quite make out what was being said.

Oh Goddess, please tell me he hadn't come to talk about what happened earlier today at his home. As far as I was concerned, the situation was over and done with, and I planned on staying as far away from that Marcus guy as possible.

It seemed Fate had a twisted sense of humor, however, when we entered the room and saw not just Knox but also the man himself . . . Marcus.

Crap. Was he going to complain to Micah about me snooping through his things?

I kept my gaze away from them both, but when Professor Knox spoke, it forced me to meet his eyes.

"I'm sorry for the intrusion tonight, but we wanted to come invite you and your family to our home for dinner this weekend." Knox stared pointedly at the man who stood rigid beside him, and all but elbowed him to speak.

Marcus cleared his throat. "It seems I owe you an apology, young Holly. You caught me off guard earlier this afternoon, and I can't imagine what you must think of me."

I instantly felt the weight of both Micah's and Sedona's gazes. I'd said nothing about the encounter with them. For all they knew, I'd handed the package to Knox at the door and returned to the bookstore quickly.

"Holly?" Micah asked, stepping toward me. I could already feel his protective energy bristling against my skin. "Did something happen that I'm not aware of?" His voice held that stern parental tone that made me want to confess everything.

Before I could answer, Marcus interrupted, coughing slightly. "If I may, Holly was waiting for Knox in my private study . . . no doubt because it was the one that had the warmest fire, and her presence startled me. Instead of acting like a gentleman, I acted out in anger and probably scared her."

I finally looked up at him and was met with a sorrowful expression. How was it possible that someone could display such complex emotions so easily from their eyes? I'd been taught to always keep my inner thoughts and feelings guarded and protected behind a psychic wall. Being around Sedona and her empathic abilities also made that shield doubly important.

Yet here was this man who wore his heart on his sleeve.

"I promise you I didn't touch anything," I stammered. The

second I did, Micah swung into full angel mode and stepped between Marcus and me.

"Did he hurt you, Holly?" The air ignited with heightened energy. "What do you have to say for your friend, Knox?"

It was Sedona who broke the tension, first placing her hand gently on Micah's arm as if to calm him. Next, she stepped around him and came face-to-face with Marcus. Nothing was said. She simply peered up into his face, searching his gaze. Then she stretched forth her hand and laid it tenderly across his cheek.

"May I?" When he nodded, she closed her eyes, drawing in a deep, fortifying breath.

Her loud gasp was the only sound that echoed in the room.

Tears tumbled over her cheeks.

What surprised me next was the man who had scared me earlier today now stood there silently—tears flowing from his own eyes.

Micah opened his mouth to say something, but it was Knox who shook his head to stop him—giving Sedona the time she needed to use her empathic powers.

A lump formed in my throat. The emotions being exchanged made the room feel heavy.

"I'm so sorry, Marcus," she finally whispered. With a tender brush of her thumb across his cheek, she reached back for Micah's hand and wrapped his arm around her. I'd seen her do this countless times before—especially when she needed to quickly ground herself from overwhelming sensations. She peered up in his concerned gaze. "His intentions are true. You have nothing to worry about with him. He means no harm."

"So, what do you think, Holly?" Micah turned to me. In fact, everyone looked over at me, waiting for me to make some decision.

"About what?" I replied, confused.

Marcus offered a soft smile. "Would you do me the honor of coming to dinner so I can make up for my poor behavior? Contrary to popular belief, I may be reclusive, but I'm sure we can find something interesting to talk about." He then turned to Sedona and Micah. "It seems silly that we haven't gotten to know each other better considering the friendship you have with my brother here."

That piqued my interest.

They were related?

"Sure," I finally answered, offering a genuine smile. "Dinner sounds like fun."

Arrangements were made and more small talk was exchanged before Micah walked the two men out. He was gone a few minutes before coming back inside, his nose already pink from the night chill.

"You sure you want to go?" he asked, leading us back to the dining room where we continued gathering up the dirty dishes.

"Of course, she's sure, Mr. Cautious. You heard her. Right, Holly?" She handed me the glasses so I could put them into the dishwasher. "We never say no to a free meal."

Micah choked on the last mouthful of water he drained from his own cup. He then smirked. "Don't pretend this is about food, Ms. Oh-My-Gosh-I-Finally-Met-The-Reclusive-Mr.-St.-James-And-Now-I-Get-To-See-Inside-His-Home." He had to pause to take in a breath. Sedona rolled her eyes at his long windedness. "Be honest. You're just dying to snoop about."

They bantered back and forth, but I was already tuning them out.

Dinner.

I sure hoped someone knew how to cook.

CHAPTER 6

*D*inner exceeded all my expectations, and Sedona was all but purring with satisfaction. It was fun watching her gawk at some of the furnishings inside Professor Knox and Marcus's home. She'd practically gushed over the artwork like I had. When Knox introduced her to just one of their libraries, Micah teased that she was about to swoon.

It was interesting to watch the adults interact with one another—how at ease they were once the awkwardness wore off. It turned out they all had a lot in common, and Sedona couldn't wait to come and explore the rare books Marcus had collected through the years.

Throughout the evening, I caught him casting me sidelong glances, but I had been content to eat the delicious meal Knox had cooked and savored each spoonful of the decadent chocolate raspberry souffle.

Once the meal was over, we all went into the room where Marcus had found me—Knox disappearing for a moment so he could bring us all warm drinks to sip on and relax. We'd barely entered the room, before Marcus cleared his throat and asked if it was okay for him to show me something outside.

Micah stood to join us, but Sedona distracted him with

comments about how our home needed new couches like this—launching them into the old debate about how many throw pillows a home actually needed.

"I hope you don't mind me pulling you away, but something caught my eye the other night, and it gave me an idea."

I followed behind Marcus as he walked down hallway after hallway, entering the biggest kitchen I'd ever seen in my life. Knox was just about to pick up the tray he'd placed the steaming cups of tea on, but with a quick smile, waved us on.

There was a door against the far wall, and with a turn of the knob, we emerged into a wintery wonderland. The backyard—if you could call it that—was unbelievably big, and unlike ours where you could see the clearly defined property boundaries marked by a wooden fence, this yard didn't seem to have an end.

"Holy cow!" I exclaimed, puffs of white fog erupting from my mouth. "Where the hell is all the snow?"

The air was frigid, and even though it was technically early spring, winter was still trying to hold on tightly, ignoring the fact that Spring Equinox had passed several days ago. That wasn't what my brain was registering as I took in the green oasis I was staring at. Trees grew tall and proud with flowering bushes, large and small, littered about the ground. Everywhere I looked I could see rich flourishing gardens that were masterfully landscaped and maintained. Colors filled my sight and the scent that filled the air was beyond heavenly.

"Are you a witch?" I blurted out. "Is it your magic that's created this private haven?" I knew it was rude to ask, but I couldn't help it. Impulse control wasn't always my strongest suit.

Pride radiated from Marcus, letting me know that he was the one responsible for it. He shrugged in response. "It's just a hobby I enjoy?"

I almost slapped his arm like I would Micah whenever he said something like that. "A hobby? This is more than some hobby. This is incredible."

He smiled, nodding his acknowledgement. "I was hoping

you'd think that." He offered his hand, and I took it without hesitation. He didn't scare me anymore. "I actually have a proposition . . . a way to make up for my behavior."

Marcus led me down a small-stoned pathway to an enchanting greenhouse a little way from the house. When he opened the door with a flourish, I gasped so loudly that I burst out laughing.

"Ask Micah . . . it's not often that I'm speechless." I stepped inside and spent the next few moments drinking everything in. Plants hung from the ceiling, and there were shelves upon shelves of different flowers and pots. This was exactly what I wanted to build in my own backyard.

That's when Marcus surprised me. "I saw some of the books in your home about herbology and one in particular—how to create your own garden. If it's okay with you, I'd like to offer up my greenhouse to you. I'll clear a space for you to work—your own bench—and maybe I could share with you some of what I've learned over the years." The man was nervous. I could see it in the way he fidgeted.

"Are you serious?" This was like a dream come true.

He nodded. "I've already spoken with Micah and Sedona, and they agree with you coming to visit . . . if you accept, of course. That invitation also extends to them. I don't want you to be afraid of me. I simply see you have an interest in the same things as me, and I thought it might be fun to learn together."

There was that vulnerability again. It was strange because there was definitely a large age difference between us, but just like me . . . I think he was simply looking for a friend.

I didn't hesitate. "Deal." I stuck out my hand to shake on it. "I can't wait to pick your brain. To new friendships."

"Initiis Novis," he murmured, nodding. "To new beginnings."

To be continued . . .

A TEENY WEENY WU

T.V. HAHN

CHAPTER 1

*A*h, spring crouches just right around the corner. While the season technically starts in a week with Spring Equinox, the weather has yet to catch up. As much as I love the beauty and peacefulness of Havenwood Falls under a bountiful blanket of snow, as I get older, I find myself far more sensitive to the cold. Apparently, so does Tang, the love of my life, who is quite a bit older than me, but he still has far more tolerance to the extent that he continues throughout the winter to do his morning walk through the woods, bundled up as he may be. I prefer to look out the kitchen window and view how the boughs of the trees bow gracefully to the ground under their burden of snow and keep my mukluks in the closet.

Which reminds me, Tang is on his morning walk right now and will definitely want a warm cup of tea when he arrives. So I put a kettle of water on to boil and set our cups, steeper, and teapot on the table. I go to the cupboard to retrieve the tea leaves, when I hear the gate to the backyard slam, and seconds later, Tang barges through the back door into the kitchen. He is out of breath, and his eyes look as if they are going to pop right out of his head.

"Siobhan! Help me! I need you to fix me something! I think I am hallucinating!" he gasps.

"My love, slow down, take your coat off, sit down, and have some tea so you can relax and tell me what you think you saw. Otherwise, I have no idea how to help you."

Tang, in such a fright, quickly doffs his coat, scarf, and gloves and plops himself down on the chair at our kitchen table, still huffing and puffing.

The kettle starts whistling, so I prepare the tea and serve him a cup. It is only after a few sips and moments later that he regains enough composure to tell me what was bothering him.

"I swear my dear, I am not making this up! I must be seeing things, and hopefully you have some potion to cure this ailment as it makes no sense."

I do my best to try to remain calm, responding, "Well, as you know, we are in Havenwood Falls, and unusual sightings are, well, not exactly uncommon."

"No, I am not speaking of supes! This is different. Giant pinecones were coming down from the mountain, and it looked as if they were heading straight to your house."

"Our house," I correct him with a smile, then I just start laughing. And laughing. And laughing.

Tang clearly grows agitated. "I know your people say laughter is the best medicine, but this is not what I need right now."

I reign in my revelry as best I can to reply, "Darling, I sent the Pixie Sisters out to gather the largest pinecones they could find, so we could glean pine nuts for Nina."

Tang says with a look of bewilderment, "Pine nuts?"

"Pine nuts are basically the seed that pine trees grow from. We call them pine nuts. In Italian they are *pignoli*, which is also the name of the cookies that Nina is going to bake for Willow Fairchild's baby shower. The pine nuts are gleaned from under the scales of the pinecones."

A gleam of enlightenment shines in his eyes, and he begins

to sip his tea in a merrier fashion. Of course, at the same time, we hear the back gate slam again, and soon after, four giant pinecones come tumbling into the kitchen through the backdoor.

"Hey, watch out!" says one of the pinecones.

"You watch out! You bumped into me!" argues another pinecone.

"Oh, be quiet you two. Let us through, and close the door!" says a third.

"Who put you in charge?" asks the first.

The fourth pinecone starts sobbing, which actually looks like a tiny hailstorm streaming out of its spiny scales.

Next thing we know, the pinecones are tumbling and now rumbling on the kitchen floor.

Tang and I take our cue and strip the Pixies of the cones, before they're destroyed, then do our best to shuffle the brawl out of the kitchen and into the parlor.

"Tang, there is so much to do with spring arriving! Aside from getting the pinecones gleaned and pine nuts cleaned, it's time to start our spring cleaning!"

"Spring cleaning? What is that?"

"Each spring we do a massive cleaning, dusting, getting rid of old stuff—not us, of course." I wink as I continue the explanation. "Removing decorations from the previous holidays, some scrubbing, cleaning the fireplace. You know, those kinds of things."

"Ah, well, I understand. I guess I have a lot to do, too. After all, I must prepare a semi-final exam for the Academy students before spring break. I have not even begun to think about it. This could take me some time."

I can only smile, knowing full well he is using this as an excuse not to help with the spring cleaning. It does not bother me since I had been spring cleaning for hundreds of years before he ever entered my life. It might very well take him longer to come up with an exam for the class than it will for me and my crew of Pixies and of course the wonderful Cyllene to prep the house for spring.

I ask Tang to carry the "giant" pinecones into the parlor for me as I carry a large empty bowl.

We find the Pixies bantering and poking one another, but otherwise they're relatively calm . . . for the Pixie Sisters, that is.

I set the bowl down in front of them and take one of the pinecones from Tang's arms and begin to show them how to remove the scales and find the pine nut. Thankfully, no one ever shut the kitchen door to the backyard, as it allows Cyllene, the wood nymph and my trusted companion, to fly in and assist the operation. Not that she can actually clean out a pinecone, but she is absolutely the best Pixie Sitter anyone could want for.

She watches attentively as I instruct the clambering clan on the process. I thank Cyllene for arriving in the nick of time to watch over the brood, so that I can attend to other tasks.

Cyllene flaps her beautiful butterfly-like wings and whisks around the room in whirling movements to let me know she is on the job. We both had come to a point that if it isn't necessary to set up our contraption to have a conversation, we can communicate easily through sign language. Well, not exactly your conventional sign language, but Cyllene knows how to give her signs to communicate to me, sometimes in a rather flamboyant fashion, like now.

With the Pixies, pinecones, and the celestial Cyllene now settled down to their tasks, I lead Tang to my salon.

Off the foyer to the left as you head to the front door is the salon. This is the room I use for my palm readings, my library of spells and other miscellany, along with the Tell All Ball and my computer.

I guess some think it might be funny that I have a computer. However, they may not be aware that I am in charge of setting up the town password, which I have the privilege of pretty much changing at will. Those people may also not be aware that I used this contraption called a computer to use Google Earth to map out my travel back to the Isle of Gwynf'l.

I show Tang how to pull up the tapestry and drop down the desk to reveal the electronic entrance to the universe—well, at least as much as the humans know of it—aka the Internet.

"Love, this salon is not used much anymore," I say. "You are more than welcome to use it as your office. Even the library. If you need room, I can put some of my books in another place."

"Siobhan, I could never be more grateful, and certainly could never find a library more enlightening than yours. It's full of wonderful background, spells, and history, and it is how you found me out and found me. I would not change a thing."

"Oh, really?"

"Well, my dear, at least not without asking you first," he replies with a twinkle in his eye that always gets me.

"So go to work! I've got cleaning to do." I close the beaded curtains behind me and return to the parlor to check on Cyllene and her wards, and what damage may have been wrought by them.

Ah, my dearest Cyllene, her colors seem to be fading more quickly now. I try relentlessly to find a way to either rejuvenate Maximus, the tree of which she is the soul, or find some way to transfer her soul. But that is almost like telling someone, "I know you have lost this one, but there are plenty more fish in the sea." (Or in this case, plenty more trees in the forest.) It might be true, but it's no consolation.

To my surprise, the parlor is in remarkably good order, and the pixies have cleaned the cones completely. As a reward, I agree to tell them a story.

"This is the story of the Easter Bunny," I start, only to be interrupted immediately by Enya.

"We don't believe in the Easter Bunny!" she states emphatically.

Aerie chimes in. "Yeah! Who would ever believe that a bunny could lay *colored* eggs!"

"You dingbat! Who would ever believe that a bunny could lay eggs, period!" Enya shoots back at her.

"I'm not a dingbat! You're a dingbat!"

I step in between the two sprites before it gets out of hand.

"Now all of you sit down. There is an Easter Bunny, and it all began on the Isle of Gwyn'fl."

They all say "Ahhh!" in unison and obediently sit on the floor, as I settle into the armchair to tell them the tale.

"Once upon a time on the Isle of Gwyn'fl, the glen was filled with bunches of bunny broods. All of the hares happily hopping through the heather. Except for two loving bunnies, Barney and Bonnie, who were unable to have a family of their own. While all the other mother and father rabbits showed off their newborn cottontails, Barney and Bonnie felt sadder than ever. Even though they were so much in love, they felt completely out of place among the frolicking furry creatures.

"So Barney and Bonnie decided to move far away from the bunny clan. They made a new home on the eastern side of the island, where no other bunnies lived. Though it was just the two of them, they were happy enough. Then one day, while rock hopping along the coastline, Bonnie found an unusual egg. The egg was multi-colored with bands of violets, pinks, blues, and yellows all swirling around its shell.

"The egg seemed to have been abandoned, and when she showed it to Barney, he agreed that they must care for it, and so they did. They brought the egg back to their bunny burrow and made a soft bed of leaves for it. Barney and Bonnie took turns keeping the egg warm by sitting on it, as they had seen birds do with their eggs.

"Then one morning, while Bonnie was taking her turn on the egg, she felt something move beneath her. She hopped up and off the egg, only to see the egg wobbling around by itself, and it rolled into a rock in the burrow. The egg cracked open, and Barney and Bonnie watched in amazement as the newborn crept out of its shell.

"It was not a bird at all! In fact, it had long floppy ears and a puff for a tail. It was a bunny! But no ordinary bunny. This bunny was as colorful as the egg it was hatched from. Barney and Bonnie scooped up the cuddly little critter and leaped for joy. They had a family!

"They moved back to the glen so they could show off their new family, and all the other bunnies were in awe of the beautiful Eastern Bunny. And sure enough, over the years, the Eastern Bunny laid the most phenomenal eggs, all kaleidoscopes of color and light. Also, over the years, as the story got told over and over again, somehow the N in Eastern got dropped, and she became known as the Easter Bunny! The end."

The Pixies all clapped for joy, then began doing bunny hops around the parlor. That should wear them out after a time.

CHAPTER 2

A long day usually leads to a long restful night's sleep. But not so much for me. Tang fell asleep almost as soon as his head hit the downy feel of the pillow. I believe he was asleep just thinking about the pillow.

For some reason, my mind is reeling. I'm not sure I can explain it. The little imps proceeded to produce a plethora of pine nuts, so that task for Nina was complete. Tang had managed to maneuver the machine we call a computer and even log on to the Internet. Goddesses and Gods behold!

So, as Tang slumbers, I lumber, tossing and turning, trying to count sheep, pixies, trees, anything. At long last, I finally fall to sleep but only to have one of my "dreams" that always seem to say something.

Even before Tang wakes, I text my personal 911 to Barbie.

TW: Long overdue for coffee. Sorry. Had a dream. Regular time?

I receive an immediate thumbs up icon from the mayor, who's also my closest friend and confidante, next to Cyllene, who can't tell anyone what I tell her anyway.

I dress quickly and quietly, not to disturb Tang, and exit the room heading down the stairs.

I'm greeted by Aerie, the little Pixie with the cloud of hair and her head in the clouds.

"Where ya goin'?"

"Gotta date with the mayor. Very important. Nothing to worry your little head about. Is that okay?"

"Sure," she says as she yawns and heads back to the parlor where all the other Pixies had fallen asleep after their pine nut pickings.

I'm extra careful to close the heavy oak door quietly, as to not alert anyone else.

Barbie is already at our customary table when I open the door to the familiar sound of the Broastful Brew, a tiny bell set atop the door. I also hear a ding-dong that sounds electronic. It makes me jump.

I eye Barbie at our table, and I can see she is chuckling over my surprise at the beeping.

Barbie's as beautiful as she always is. This morning, her hair, a very wispy bouffant of a light purplish color, sits atop her head.

"Nice color. What do you call it?" I ask her as I pull up the chair and add a cushion under me to sit up higher.

"It's lilac. My lilacs will be blooming soon, and I want to be the Mother Earth to greet them properly."

"I like it! It suits you. It suits me, too." I smile.

Mabel brings our usual order to our table.

"Mabel, where is Mat?" I ask. Mat, my nephew, who works here and married Nina had been the one to serve us for the past few years.

"Dahling!" she starts in her southern drawl. "Duncha know? Mat and Nina have a helluva a lot going on."

"I know Nina wants to make Pignoli for the baby shower, so we have been working on helping her. Is there something else?"

"Not for me to say, sugar cakes. But as I see it, all's right down south."

Mabel departs, and I think I have a huge question mark over my head as I turn my attention back to my friend Barbie.

She reads my expression immediately as good friends do.

"Don't go all ADD on me, Siobhan. You called me here. What's up? You had a dream?"

"So sorry, Barbie, my bad!" I continue, "Yes, I had a dream. It wasn't exactly a nightmare, but I think it has a lot of symbolism that I am just not getting."

"So spit it out!" She sips her latte.

I describe to my friend and oneirocritic what transpired in my dream.

"I was surrounded by my family and the town, all holding hands in a circle. My family stood all together. There was Mat, Nina, the Pixies, Grenfold and Coralie, you, Cyllene, even HimaLaLa. We all stood in the town square. It looked like we were preparing for a spring celebration." Then I hesitate.

Barbie smiles her perfect politician smile, and then she lets it go. "You have to continue. You know, as well as I, that there is just a little bit more to this dream."

I so wish I had hair as great as hers, so when I bow my head in shame, such hair would cover my sorrowfulness.

"You are right. I am sorry for not getting directly to the point. So here was this big family and great community, but suddenly there is this big hole in the middle. It is not the fountain in the square. I can't even describe it. It's like a vortex leading down to an abyss or a tornado pulling everything up from the ground, but what has left caused a black hole. I just don't get it. This is probably the first time my life feels complete. Tang is in my life. He is the most wonderful man, and I love him so much. The Pixie Sisters are, well, the Pixie Sisters—adorable, aggravating, gregarious, aggressive. I am so happy Mat found me. It is wonderful to have more family nearby, and that he even fell in love with Nina, my friend for some time. That the Pixies, Mat, and I were able to bring Coralie here and place her in Peacock Lake and even reunite her with Gruff, you know, I mean Grenfold, who was Gruff, but now Grenfold again."

"Teeny! Oops, I mean Siobhan, you are rambling. Get to the point."

"Well, that is my point. What does this big hole, vortex, abyss, black hole, or whatever mean?"

Barbie, in her grand but not ostentatious manner sips her coffee. She takes a deep breath then replies, "You already know the answer. Look around you! You have everything and everybody you need. You have family, but all of your family are . . . so to speak, extended family. I am not one to talk, but it looks to me that you have found your true love, and it may be time for you to look to the future."

"What? Tang and I are old, like really old, like way older than you! Havenwood Falls is good enough for me, and I am pretty sure it is good enough for Tang. I don't even know what you mean, look to the future."

"How do you know it's good enough for Tang? Yes, he has an ancient past, but he got here taking over his great-great-great —okay I forgot how many greats—nephew's body, which he used to get here and *find* none other than *you!* If that's not the future, then nothing is."

"Barbie, I'm still not getting it. What does it mean? What is the hole?"

"I love you, Teeny Weeny! Siobhan! You keep describing it is a hole, but it is the *whole*. You need to embrace it all. Make it a *whole* family. You know how, you just have to look to the past to find the future. You and Tang are meant for each other. I'm glad both of you are here in Havenwood Falls."

We left the Broastful Brew as the ting-a-ling of the shop bell announces our departure and the arrival of a bunch of newcomers.

I wander back to my little townhome trying to figure out what Barbie meant. Usually, she's much more direct, but this time, she was quite elusive. That's not like her.

To my amazement, the Pixies, under the guidance of Cyllene, have actually filled the bowl with pine nuts, and the scales of the pine cones have been tossed into the fireplace, rendering a comforting aroma of conifers.

Mat and Nina are sitting in the parlor, waiting for my arrival, which to me is rather strange, since I'm the first to wake and the first to move, not to mention, first to get to the coffee shop. I wonder how long I was with Barbie.

"Hello, family!" I say, but really it is more with a question mark in my mind.

Mat speaks first. "We have an announcement to make. Nina and I have chosen to start a family! "

"Ahem." Nina clears her throat and conveniently draws the attention away from Mat, who is not very good at public speaking. "What we mean, is we love our family! They are so magnifico, and we are so magnifico together. We are simpatico! Okay, so what we mean is we want to have a bambino! Capiche?"

The Pixies cheer in such a tremendous hooplah that I'm afraid fireworks would start spurting out of the fireplace. They have no problem translating what Nina is saying. Neither do I.

In unison, the Pixie Sisters also add, "Make sure you make enough cookies with the Pig-a-ma-thingies for HimaLaLa," and with that, roll into a fit of laughter, soon to become a wrestling match for sure.

I do not even know what to say to Tang. We just dressed for bed, and comfortably, we look at one another, and as we usually do, we hold each other's hand as we fall asleep.

But I do not fall asleep. I keep thinking about Barbie, the hole, the whole, what is all of this? What is the past to look to the future? It means something but what?

I decide that tomorrow morning I will go to Peacock Lake and speak to my brother. Maybe he would have some insight.

CHAPTER 3

My brother Grenfold, bless his soul and heart . . . Many centuries ago, our father turned him into a troll because my brother dared to love a mermaid, Coralie. For way too many years, my own brother was known as Gruff the Troll. While Father was alive, I had no choice other than to watch over my brother and try as I could to help him to know I was always going to be his sister.

I enjoy the walk up to Peacock Lake. There is a wonderful path first walked upon by Native Americans that lived here long before we found Havenwood Falls. In fact, there are descendants that still inhabit the town. The trail that leads to Peacock Lake does not really lead to Peacock Lake. You enter first by a grand trail that is marked by an age-old bristlecone pine that had been struck down by lightening about six generations or more ago. That tree "stump" is Maximus. That tree harbors the soul that I know as Cyllene.

She follows me along the trail that continues to the triple falls. The Triplets, as I've dubbed them, pour into Peacock Lake, and are more commonly known as Small Falls. The name has nothing to do with the size, even though all three are so much smaller than Havenwood Falls's Great Falls.

I stand by the edge of Peacock Lake, rendering as best I can the summoning call that can be heard, and most likely should *only* be heard, by Coralie.

A splash of tail announces her arrival, and by her side of course is Grenfold. He has vowed never to leave her side again, and with that vow, Coralie bestowed him with the gift of merfolk, the ability to breathe underwater.

I tell them both about Mat and Nina, holding off on purpose to describe my dream. After all, this is family news. Great news in fact!

Both the beautiful red-headed mermaid and her handsome prince wallow in the lake with enormous grins on their mer-faces.

"What's with you two?" I ask.

Coralie winks at me, but my brother takes the cue. "Siobhan, it's nearly spring. We are not surprised that Mat and Nina are planting a seed. It seems that Coralie and I are doing the same. Or should I say, have done the same."

"Oh, my Goddesses and Gods! You are going to have mer-babies?"

The couple just continue with their grinning but add very enthusiastic nodding of their heads to the mix.

"That's great! I am so happy for you both. You both deserve so much happiness after so many generations of heartbreak. I was going to make a potion for Nina, to ensure the health of the newborn to be, but it seems I will have to make a double batch."

I can't help myself. I start jumping on one foot and then the other. It's my happy dance.

"Was there anything else you wanted to tell us?" Coralie asks thoughtfully.

"Oh, no. Just wanted to spread the news, and now I have even more to share." I don't want to ruin their moment with my own troubles. I will work it out. I hope.

I start to head back down the trail, with Cyllene yammering

away in such a small and speedy voice that I never can make out what she's saying without our megaphone device.

"Silly Annie, I'm just going to ripple home. I will meet you there."

More yammering, but this time I know she's trying to correct me on the pronunciation of her name, See-lee-knee. I ignore her as I begin my ripple. The air around me flutters then becomes waves as I drift into the ripple with ease.

I've explained many times that there is a stipple in the ripple. Time can move forward or backward but rarely sideways. In this case, I arrive at my house at sunset. Cyllene's already at my townhome, impatiently waiting my arrival as she flits back and forth between the parlor, salon, and kitchen.

I ripple into my backyard, a wonderfully secluded garden behind the row of businesses with their upper-floor apartments on Main Street, where I feel safe that no one sees my coming or going, and I enter through the back door into the kitchen. Cyllene is just flitting back into the kitchen and begins her yammering again, but this time her sign language is clear. She's banging herself up against the cabinet that holds our communication mechanism. As I set up our makeshift PA, Cyllene alights on the table, anxiously flapping her all too gorgeous wings, the bright opalescent green of them sending rays of light bouncing throughout the kitchen.

"Why didn't you tell Grenfold about your dream? You wouldn't go all the way up there just to tell them that Mat and Nina are going to start a family. After all, Mat could've just flown up there and made his own announcement. What's with that?"

"I know, Silly Annie, but once they made their announcement, it wasn't right for me to bother them with my own trivial affairs. They deserve their day in the sun, or in the lake, as the case may be."

Cyllene, of course, harrumphs at my calling her Silly Annie, but we both ignore it this time, mainly because we hear Tang calling from the salon.

"Teeny, is that you?" he starts then clears his throat with an ahem and speaks again, "I mean Siobhan. You are home?"

I giggle under my breath, understanding that Tang has now immersed himself into Havenwood Falls, befriended so many of the residents, has been working with all the teachers, and of course all of his students. They all have called me Teeny Weeny since I don't remember when. It's natural for him to pick up the nickname. I really don't mind at all. I actually find it a bit charming, like he's charming.

I respond back that I'm home and try gracefully to depart from Cyllene's demonstrative admonitions.

I walk into the salon to find Tang at the round table in the center of the room, books strewn all over the tabletop, but he's intent on the one in front of him.

"Ah! There you are! Come look! I was perusing your shelves of spells, potions, incantations, legends, etc. and found this!" Tang holds up a large volume with a dark green leather cover and gold lettering. "It's a book called *Faerie's Guide to Gardening*. With spring on our heels, I thought you might find this helpful. I know your garden is prolific, but perhaps you may want to add something new? I saw the crocuses blooming as they shed the last of the light blanket of snow the other day."

"You did?" I ask suspiciously, since the other day he'd come storming into the kitchen in a pinecone-induced fright.

"Yes, well, I mean when I left for my morning walk. It made me think of all the plum blossom trees and tiny orchids that always bloomed this time of year in my own homeland."

"I haven't looked at this book in years. I have gleaned through it so many times in the past and just became used to tilling, planting, watering, and growing all the flowers, vegetables, ivies, and even weeds, without thinking about it."

Tang opens the book to a page he had placed his purple tassel to mark. The heading reads, "The Flower of Life."

"I think you should read this, my dear, in light of Mat and Nina's proclamation," he states as he hands me the *Guide*.

"You might be right, considering I also got such word from Grenfold and Coralie that she is now full of roe."

I take the book into my hands and begin to read the chapter he marked.

The Flower of Life

Spring Fae who are borne from the Flower of Life, granted to us by the Goddesses of Spring, must understand that with each blooming Fae, they shall also be born with a seed of the Flower of Life. It is their destiny to ensure that the earth will flourish and thrive, as all its creatures shall too.

It is earth, air, sun, and rain that nourish, but the seed itself must be planted. Life is not life without love. Therefore, the Goddess of Spring, Brid, blessed the seeds that they shall bring forth new life whenever true love has planted the seed.

I know the seed this chapter is talking about. I have kept it safe in a special container since my mother had given it to me on my tenth bloom day. She explained that the seed must be preserved by me until I am ready and have found a love that will help me to make it blossom.

I remember I joked with her about the Goddess Brid and how her name sounds as if she were a bride. My mother laughed, her gentlest, joyous laugh and replied, "Well, in a way that's true. Brid is married to the earth, sun, air, and rain. It is with all of these elements that she is able to produce the miraculous life that we see all around us. From the tiniest lichen to the largest mammoths, she helped to create it all. She also has placed us in charge of preserving the legacy. It is our task to continue so that we and all that live among us thrive, endure, and survive. Bless Brid and all the Goddesses and Gods that have made this possible."

"Bless them all!" I'd responded in my youthfulness.

The truth is not a laughing matter. My mother nearly died when she gave birth to my brother Grenfold. My father refused to allow her to get pregnant again. This broke her heart, as she wanted more than anything to have a girl. So my mother prayed to Goddess Brid to help her have another baby fae. Because of my mother's loyalty and devotion to the Goddess, she blessed her with the Flower of Life, my birth flower.

Alas, a true love I had never found, over many hundreds of years. That is until now. I would have thought it impossible, but bless my Goddess Brid, true love thrives, as well as all the living things now on earth. Tang has also conveniently handed me my *Guide to Gardening* marked with this particular chapter. There might be more to his wizardry that I am not aware.

I think there will be much more to talk about than just holding hands when we go to bed tonight.

CHAPTER 4

*W*ith the house now peaceful and quiet with the Pixies back in their den with HimaLaLa and Cyllene roosting with Maximus, Tang and I pad quietly up the stairs to our bedroom. We silently dress for bed, then settle in under the down comforter. I start to reach for his hand, but he draws it away unexpectedly.

"What is wrong, my dear?" I ask quizzically.

"You have been holding something back. I wasn't quite sure what it was, but it became more apparent when Mat and Nina informed us of their intent and even more so when you returned with your brother's disclosure of their upcoming offspring. You seemed happy but somehow agitated. Then I showed you the *Guide to Gardening,* and you seemed to back off even more. I think there is something you still need to tell me."

I gulp down my guilt. He, of course, is right. I have not told him about the "seed." I roll over to my bedstand and withdraw a very small wooden box that I keep in the drawer. I set it on the bed between us.

At first, Tang wrinkles his nose, not sure what to make of this box. Then his eyes open so wide, it reminds me of his entrance the other day when he thought he was being chased by giant pinecones, except this time with amazement and even fascination.

I start to open the box, but he stops me.

"Wait! The runes inscribed on this box are so similar to the ancient Chinese characters that symbolize life 'Qi' and the yin yang. Tell me what I should expect or am I expecting too much?"

"Inside this box is a seed. When I was born, there was a seed that came with my blossom. That seed was preserved by my mother in a special glass container, sealed with a gold filament and placed in this box. The runes are so much like the words we just read about the Flower of Life. This is my seed for our Flower of Life. I could not plant it until, I think now, because of you. But only if you want."

Tang is silent for what seems to me like an eternity. His expression changes from incomprehension to comprehension, then to what appears as sadness then happiness. I am not sure what his response would be, but I know I am happy that I'm sharing this with him and sharing my life with him.

"Siobhan, just let me know what you need me to do. When I first met you, from the moment I smelled your scent in the Broastful Brew, shared tea at Michaela's inn and we walked through the observatory, and even when we had the face-off as enemies, or so we thought, I knew you were the woman for me. A tremendous force in a Teeny Weeny body. I have lived centuries only hoping that this day would come, so whatever we can do to continue this love, let's do it."

I can do nothing else but hug this wonderful man as wholeheartedly as I can possibly muster. I think I almost crush him.

"Tang, we have much to do in the morning. Let's sleep well tonight. I think the hole or whole in my dream is about to be resolved. I love you."

"Hole? I don't know what that means but I love you too, my

dear." Then we kiss and roll over, and I turn off the Tiffany-style lamp on my bedside.

As soon as the sun sheds its first light through the bedroom window, I am totally awake. I have slept so well and am so anxious to start the day, this day. I grab the small wooden box I had shown Tang last night, fit my feet into my slippers, don a robe, and pad down the steps to the kitchen to start tea and breakfast.

Today is going to be planting day. I am so excited. I now understand what Barbie meant. There is a hole in the family, one that needs to be filled by Tang and myself, to make the entire family whole. Looking out the window, I see the sun shining brightly into my garden, beckoning me. Though a faint layer of snow appears in spots here and there, it is clear that most has thawed, and by mid-morning it should be perfect for sowing our seed.

Tang comes into the kitchen fully dressed, with the *Guide to Gardening* in hand. I pour us the tea I had brewed and place a plate of toast and the honey pot between us.

"I read here," he begins, "that there is a spell that we must say together before we plant the seed, and then we must follow it precisely. Do you have the tools we need?"

"Of course, right under the sink I keep the trowel, claw, and watering can," I answer. "As soon as I finish my tea, I will get dressed then we will go in the backyard, and I will show you where we will plant."

Once dressed, I pull the items we need from underneath the sink, and we both exit the back door and enter the garden.

Right below the kitchen window is a row of tiny crocuses in bloom. I point to a spot between the blossoms, indicating that this will be the place for our seedling.

Tang reads the spell aloud.

Lovers' hands shall toil
and together till the soil.
Dig a hole into the ground,
bury the seed then tamp it down.
Moisten the plot you did sow,
soon from love a life will grow.

"First, we must till the ground together, hand in hand," I instruct as I lift the gardening claw.

Tang wraps his warm hand around mine, and we bend down to loosen the earth. That task complete, Tang catches on right away and picks up the trowel. This time I place my small hands on top of his as he digs a hole into the soil.

I wave my hand over the miniature wooden box, and a lid suddenly pops open. Like the box my wand is kept in, it operates by fae vibrations. I remove the small glass container that's adorned with a crystal flower on top. I hold the bottle up toward the sun, letting the rays begin to warm the gold filament, then gently touch the floral lid. The gold melts and drips down the sides of the vial as I carefully remove the crystal topper. I gently tap the seed out of its container and into its new bed. Together we cover the cherished seed with the earth and tamp it down.

We walk over to the water pump near the gate, and I hold the can as Tang pumps the precious fluid that would help our blossom to thrive.

We moisten the spot where our plant is now bedded, and both step back in unison.

"Now what?" Tang asks. "How long does this take? Is it like human gestation, or normal germination period?"

"Well, we've done everything we were supposed to. The spell says 'soon,' but in fae time that could be a day, a week, or even a year. We just have to tend to it with all our love and wait and see."

Just at that moment, the Pixie Sisters come skipping through the back gate.

"What's you doin'?" asks Aerie.

"Just a little gardening," I reply.

"Ooh, what did you plant?" queries Tierri.

"It's a surprise!" says Tang.

"Surprise! Surprise! We all love surprises!" They all start singing and dancing around in a circle.

It does not happen in a day, nor a week or even two. We tend to it every morning, with loving care and tender prayers. Then just about the time the cherry tree in the backyard has begun to bud, I see a small green sprout pop up from the ground we had planted.

I run in as quickly as I can to tell Tang the news, and he joins me in the backyard. I think he's more excited than I am. But not for long.

"That's it? This little sprig?" he wonders aloud. Then he kind of looks a little guilty.

"Just give it a little more time. This means we have done everything right, and our love is growing right here before our very eyes."

From that moment, that tiny sprout seems to grow quite fast. We keep constant watch on it day and night.

On May Day, a bloom not fully opened appears at the top of the stem of our once tiny sprout. I let Tang know that I think it's time. It's about to blossom, and we don't want to miss one minute of it, hoping and praying for the Goddess's blessings.

We stand in front of that flower-to-be most of the morning, when again the Pixies arrive in full throng, waving their colored ribbons in preparation for their May Pole dance. When they see we're watching the plant, they all settle down and squat close by to get a Pixie's eye view of the blooming of the flower. They know not what to expect, and neither do we really. I just hope I have preserved the seed well enough and that our love was fertile enough, but only the blossoming of this lovely flower will tell.

Then the miracle occurs. The bud sitting atop the stem begins to open its petals, slowly, luxuriously, almost as if it's stretching after waking up from a long peaceful sleep.

And in the bloom is a little faerie baby, eyes still shut, but tossing its tiny head from side to side. There's a little bell that almost looks like a bluebell on top of her head, and it rings a soft, sweet note with each nod.

"Look!" squeals Ushka. "It's a Teeny Weeny Wu!"

They all start giggling, and Aerie pipes up, "We should call her Ting-a-Ling for the sound of her bell."

"You're a ding-a-ling!" Enya retorts. "They have to name her."

"I'm not a ding-a-ling! You're a ding-dong!" Aerie defends herself. Then comes the brawl.

Tang quickly grabs up the four Pixies by the napes of the necks and scurries them away from our newly bloomed daughter. After scolding them, he tells them they must now behave, as they will have a lot of responsibility to help me take care of the new arrival.

When he returns, I look at him thoughtfully, then say, "You know, I think Ting is a good name. Tang and Ting Wu. What do you think?"

He smiles and nods as I pluck the tiny faeling still wrapped in her petals and hold her gently in my hands as Tang puts his arm around me. We walk into the house, our home, and our family.

The Pixies traipse in behind us, singing the witch doctor song, "Ting Tang Walla Walla Bing Bang" and leave a rainbow of strewn ribbons all over the backyard.

A SPRINKLE OF FATE

E.J. FECHENDA

A SPRINKLE OF FATE

I stood in wonder, taking in the extravagant decorations. The outdoor patio at the Creekwood Country Club had been transformed into an English garden that rivaled that of any country estate. My mom and my aunt Rhiannon, owners of Fairy Tale Florists, had outdone themselves.

"What do you think, Willow?" my mom asked, wrapping her arm around my hips and tucking me close to her side. Our heads touched, and I breathed in her familiar scent—lavender and vanilla.

"It's absolutely gorgeous, Mom." My throat was thick with tears. Damn hormones had my emotions all over the place.

"Nothing but the best for my baby girl and her baby," she said before releasing me. "I just need to adjust that topiary as it looks a little crooked."

I couldn't see anything wrong with it but trusted my mom's eyes. She was the professional.

As she wandered off, I took a moment for myself and closed my eyes, tilted my face toward the sun, and breathed in the fresh mountain air. The weather had worked in our favor, and while it was a little chilly, it was still warm for early spring. The heating lamps scattered around the patio didn't have to be turned on, and the parkas and snow boots had been retired for another season, except for skiing, as the mountains that circled the box canyon town of Havenwood Falls were still capped with glistening snow.

"Holy fairies, Willow, if you get any bigger, I won't be able to hug you properly," my cousin Paisley teased. I opened my eyes right before she gave me an enthusiastic hug and patted my baby bump.

"Watch it, Paise, this will be you one day."

Her fair cheeks lit up with a bright blush, almost as pink as her hair, as she furiously shook her head in denial. "School first, career second, possibly marriage, and then, way, way, way down the road, I might consider some spawn."

I chuckled at her denial. I felt the same way until I met Chase and my world changed in an instant. Now I was pregnant with my second child and already thinking about adding a third. The way Paisley and her boyfriend, Timber, looked at each other with stars and hearts emojis in their eyes, made it obvious to everyone they were in love, but with me being an empath, I was able to perceive just how deep and serious their feelings for each other ran. Their souls were practically entwined, and the love they emitted when together, told me Paisley might be settling down sooner than she thought.

A commotion by the entrance to the patio drew my attention, and as soon as I turned to look, I saw my daughter Arabella running toward me with her arms stretched wide. She barreled into my legs with an oomph and practically knocked me on my ass. She was almost five years old and a hurricane of energy.

"Ara, easy on your mommy," Reeve chastised as she approached, preceded by her own baby bump. I grinned at her, recognizing the exhaustion that marked her pale face, as I wore the same marks. It wasn't easy being pregnant with a toddler to chase after. Reeve's daughter was a year and a half younger than

Arabella, and the two had become thick as thieves. Whenever Reeve visited from Denver, we arranged playdates for our daughters. Soon the two were running toward the water fountain located at the edge of the patio. The soft rolling hills of the golf course stretched out behind the gray stone fountain.

"I'll keep an eye on them," Paisley promised and ran off after the little troublemakers. Reeve's sister Aster, former manager of my shop Coffee Haven, arrived behind her sister, carrying her sleeping son. His russet hair stuck up in a halo of uncontrollable curls, and a dribble of drool connected his mouth to his mom's shirt.

"Lucky for us, this demon just cried himself into a nap. He should be good for an hour or two," Aster whispered. "Fingers crossed."

I snorted and shook my head. Their child was one hundred percent mountain lion shifter and not a demon, but after surviving the terrible twos, I knew what she meant. "Famous last words, my dear friend."

Aster and Reeve left to go find seats at a table, and I walked to the entrance to greet people as they arrived. Guests flowed in through the door, a mix of family and friends, both human and supernatural. Most of the town's founding families were represented. Since I was the great-granddaughter of Elsmed Fairchild, one of the founding members, this baby shower was kind of a big deal.

First to arrive were the Augustines. Mathilde, who was one of the leaders of the Luna Coven, her daughters-in-law Ronya and Ami, followed by Ami's daughters, my friend Harlow and her younger sister Taylor. Harlow squealed when she saw me and pulled me into a hug, acting like it had been months since she last saw me when we had just worked together at Coffee Haven the day before.

"Reyna tagged along with us. We both had a late night at the clubhouse," Harlow said with a wink as Reyna pulled me into a hug. I could only imagine. Both Harlow and Reyna's mates were part of the local motorcycle club and the parties at the MC clubhouse were legendary. There were even rumors of an underground fight club.

They left to find seats right before the Beaumonts arrived, Addie along with her mom, Lyra, and grandmother, Saundra, also members of the Luna Coven. I watched to see where they would sit since Reyna was dating Lyra's ex, and I wanted to avoid any potential awkwardness. When they chose a table on the opposite side of the dining area from Reyna, I let out a small sigh of relief, and turned to greet my next guests, smiling when two moroi vampires, Michaela and her sister Aurelia, stepped onto the patio.

"Willow, you have no idea how annoyed Elsmed was that he couldn't attend your shower. At the last Court meeting he couldn't stop grumbling about the men being excluded. I told him to get over it," Michaela said with a grin, causing faint laugh lines to crinkle around her unusual gray-green eyes, which were a signature feature of the Moroi.

"He just hates missing out on a chance to eat free food," I replied. My great-grandfather had accumulated significant wealth over the past centuries, and while he was stern and instilled fear in many, he was also known for his generosity. But he could also be quite the miser.

Letitia and Macy Blackstone, representing yet another Old Family, pushed through the patio door seconds after Michaela and her sister went to sit with the Beaumonts.

My lower back was beginning to ache from standing, and I swore my ankles were now cankles, but I couldn't see past my belly to confirm. Why was I contemplating more children? I had to be insane. Just then my baby kicked, and I swore she hit a kidney that time. I winced just as Sedona Matthews arrived with Holly, who had practically become a permanent fixture at the bookstore Sedona owned, which was located right next door to Coffee Haven.

"Hey, are you okay?" Sedona asked, clearly sensing my

discomfort. As a fellow empath, picking up on what others were feeling wasn't easy to avoid.

"I'm fine. Chanell is feisty today. I think she knows this party is for her and doesn't want to be ignored. I fear she's going to be quite the diva." I rubbed my hand over my belly in a soothing motion, sending calming energy into my womb.

"And you should be sitting down," Paisley said, appearing at my side. I quickly scanned the area looking for Arabella. "She's fine. Your mom has her."

I breathed out a sigh of relief and allowed my cousin to guide me to a large, padded chair that resembled a throne, which was positioned near the gift table. Paisley was a healer, and as soon as I was seated, she knelt down by my feet.

"Bow to your queen," I said, making my voice haughty and deep.

Paisley rolled her violet eyes and picked up one of my feet. Her hands glowed, and the swollen feeling in my ankle vanished. She then applied the same treatment to my other ankle, and I sighed in relief. "Thanks, cousin. I feel like a balloon."

"Well, you are ready to burst, so it's understandable." She pulled a small, matching padded stool out from beneath my throne and propped my feet on it for some slight elevation. "I'll bring you some tea. Just sit and relax, let people come to you. My dad advised me to tell you that."

"So, doctor's orders?" Paisley's dad, my uncle Jasper, was a doctor who practiced at the medical center and had helped deliver Arabella.

"You got it!" she said with a grin before leaving to fetch me a cup of tea. So, I sat there, like a queen and let my friends and family come see me. My belly received more rubs than a Buddha statue before my mom and aunt called out for everyone to take a seat.

The twenty or so tables were decorated with fine porcelain tea sets, inlaid with gold accents, and bouquets that spilled cascades of colorful blossoms onto the cream silk tablecloths.

Each place setting contained a gift for the attendees. My mom and aunt had created little pouches that were made of bio-degradable and nutrient rich papyrus which contained seeds for daisies. Daisies were symbolic of new beginnings, a perfect way to usher in spring and celebrate new life. All anyone had to do was bury the entire envelope in soil. I was looking forward to seeing patches of yellow daisies in the coming months. They'd be like little bursts of sunshine.

Speaking of sun, I was thankful for the little canopy over my chair to block the sun for even though it was a chilly, early spring day, I was basically a little furnace with the baby on board and needed all the shade I could get.

My mom pushed a tea cart over next to me and took a seat in a chair beside mine. The tea cart contained a tiered platter full of finger sandwiches and tiny pastries. I recognized miniature versions of the blueberry scones we sold at Coffee Haven and quickly snagged one.

"Roxy made those," my mom said as she piled food onto her plate. I looked across the patio and located the cougar shifter who worked part-time at the Coffee Haven shop we opened on the campus of the Sun and Moon Academy, a college located inside Mount Alexa. Roxy was sitting at a table and talking with Amanda George, my manager's wife. Amanda was one of the few humans in attendance, which meant this was a strictly non-magical event. With several of the female members of the Court of the Sun and the Moon, the governing council for all things supernatural in our town, in attendance, everyone was expected to be on their best behavior.

As the afternoon wore on, I reclined against the padded cushion with a hand resting on my belly, more swollen than ever since I had eaten half my weight in pastries. Happiness buzzed in the air. Occasionally I'd pick up on a whiff of anxiety, but overall, everyone was in a good mood, and that let my empathic nature relax. Crowds were always challenging. Despite taking measures to block emotions, I could never fully turn it off. I used my abilities to monitor people and determine who might be on the verge of doing something dangerous or harmful. If I sensed something bad, I had to alert someone on the Court or Sheriff Kasun.

"Do you need anything?" my mom asked, as she refilled her teacup. The gold leafing glinted in the sunshine.

"I'm good, Mom. Thank you for this. This baby shower is amazing."

"Sprinkle."

"What?" I asked, squinting my turquoise eyes at her in confusion.

"Technically, a baby shower for the second child is called a sprinkle."

"Really? Who comes up with these things, anyway?"

My mom chuckled and shook her head, her chestnut bob bouncing with the movement. "The Internet?"

I laughed at her response and groaned as Chanell kicked my side.

"Ooomph. I think that was my spleen this time." I winced and rubbed my side.

"You were a big kicker. Thought for sure you'd become a soccer player, but you never liked sports. Well, aside from skiing and ice skating."

"Not competitive sports. All the aggression and anxiety over winning or losing?" I shuddered at the memory of attending Friday night football games when I was in high school. Those football games were a concentrated cesspit of emotions and chaotic energy I hadn't fully come into my abilities until my senior year, but my empathic nature had started to develop earlier during my junior year, triggered by what is now referred to as the "Vampire Massacre of 2005."

"Hmmm . . . that's true. I never thought of that." She gave me a contemplative look before squeezing my hand. "I won't pretend to understand what being an empath is like, but if you ever get overwhelmed, you know you can come to me, right?

Motherhood has its challenges, and you're going to need to be prepared when your girls are teenagers. Emotions are going to be flying around so fast, you'll get whiplash."

"Ugh, this one is still incubating. Can we not talk about them being teenagers already?" I said and swallowed past a lump in my throat that had formed at the thought, blinking away unshed tears. Arabella had proven just how quickly kids grew up. It seemed like yesterday when she was born. I wasn't ready. Holy fairies, I was a mess. Stupid hormones.

My mom patted my hand in understanding before tapping a spoon against her teacup to get everyone's attention. She announced it was time to open presents and stood to grab one. The gift table next to our chairs was full of gift bags and wrapped presents that covered the whole spectrum of pastel pink, green, purple, and yellow.

As we were approaching the last of the gifts, I had already accumulated a lifetime supply of diapers and baby wipes. An assortment of outfits and onesies, story books, and toys rounded out the mix. Sherry, another Coffee Haven regular, had made a gorgeous blanket she knitted out of the softest white yarn. Just as my mom was getting ready to hand me another gift bag, the air around us shimmered, and the pressure changed in my ears.

Suddenly a portal appeared near the fountain and a beautiful woman stepped out, escorted by . . . my husband?

The woman wore an empire waisted gown that accentuated her breasts, and the cobalt blue material pooled around her feet. She had white, silvery blond hair, that was very similar to mine, but where mine fell in a long curtain to my waist, hers was piled on top of her head in an elaborate updo of braids. Nestled on top of the coils of braids was a rose gold crown inlaid with a rainbow of gems. She had used a glamour to appear human except for her ears. The tops formed into high points, a classic feature of the fae.

Her arm was tucked inside my husband's, and he regarded her with an awed reverence that I did not like one bit. The crown told me who this woman was, and while I knew my husband worked for her, I had never met her before. Chase's job as a liaison between the Seelie Court and Havenwood Falls required him to spend a lot of time in Faerie. Oftentimes he spent weeks away in the other realm. I never minded before, but seeing this stunningly beautiful woman on his arm made all those long absences from home a little difficult to be understanding about.

I zeroed in on the pair to get a read on their emotions. Fortunately for Chase, all I detected was reverence and a little bit of fear, but no lust or love. From the queen, I detected absolutely nothing. She was a complete void, and that shocked me. Her bright, spring green eyes met mine, and she winked. The Seelie Queen actually winked at me before she wove gracefully around the tables full of seated guests to approach me. How she managed to do that with Chase still by her side was impressive.

"One of the perks of being royalty, my dear, is that I can shield myself when abilities are trying to be used toward me. Those that are subtle and not so subtle." This time she gave me a pointed look, and I lowered my gaze, my cheeks blazing with heat when I blushed.

"My apologies, your highness. Or is it your majesty? Should I curtsy? I can try, but my body might object." I shifted forward in my chair with a grunt, belly leading the way, and attempted to stand. This is when I realized how it seemed as though our roles were reversed. I was sitting on a replica of a throne, and she was before me like a subject. Sweat broke out along my brow as I wondered if this would be seen as even more disrespectful.

The queen laughed. Even her laugh was lovely, like wind chimes coaxed by a gentle breeze. "Please relax, my dear. You're not at Court so certain rules don't apply, and I apologize for not following proper protocol with this unsanctioned visit." She turned and dipped her head toward the members of the Court of the Sun and the Moon who were scowling at her. "But I have a message to deliver regarding your unborn child, which could be considered a gift." She paused and faced me again, her eyebrows pulled together, causing a crease to form on her otherwise perfectly smooth forehead. "Or not."

I immediately sought out my husband, and he looked just as surprised and overwhelmed as I did at this revelation, which let me know he wasn't informed as to what this surprise visit was about. A wave of anxiety from him washed over me, and I clenched the arms of the chair, bracing myself for the queen's "message." What the faeries was going on?

Chase whispered in the queen's ear, and she nodded, pulling her arm free. He immediately crossed over to me and pulled me into his arms like I weighed nothing. Within seconds, he was sitting in the chair and I was on his lap, his arms wrapped protectively around me and our unborn daughter. He nuzzled against my neck and placed a soft kiss on the patch of sensitive skin right below my ear. He was comforting me as much as my being in his arms reassured him.

"What is this message?" he demanded, his Scottish brogue extremely pronounced, indicating he was feeling just as uneasy as I was.

My mom and aunt had come to stand beside my chair on either side, in somewhat defensive stances, and the queen's eyes lit up when she saw my mom's empty seat.

"Oh, do you mind?" She glided over and sat down with the poise of a ballerina. She poured herself some tea and breathed in the aromatic steam, probably checking to make sure it didn't contain any lemon, since we fae were highly allergic, before taking a sip. She then proceeded to pick up a blueberry scone and popped the whole thing in her mouth. She daintily chewed and swallowed. "Mmmmm, these are delicious," she said then wiped her pouty lips free of any crumbs with a cloth napkin.

I stared at her incredulously. Was she prolonging the suspense deliberately or was she completely obtuse and unaware of the tension lacing the air? Everyone's attention was riveted on the powerful being as she continued to snack, helping herself to a white chocolate raspberry mini muffin next. I so did not have the patience for this and shifted on Chase's lap, but he lowered his hands to my hips and gave them a squeeze, reminding me to stay calm. I glared at him and let out a huff, but he just leaned forward and gave me a quick kiss infused with so much love and concern that I settled down. How he worked for this infuriating fae was beyond me.

A few more tension-laced minutes passed, and the swirl of emotions bombarding me from my friends and family, along with my own precarious emotional state, tipped me over the edge.

"Oh, for faeries sake, you said you have a message for Chase and me. Care to share, your majesty?" I snapped, and Chase gripped my hips even tighter, like he thought I was going to launch myself at the queen. I was tempted. Apparently, pregnancy brought out an inner feistiness. Usually I was calm and serene. Not at this moment.

A few gasps followed my outburst, and I heard someone say "Oh shit." The queen didn't respond. She just set her napkin down next to the tray of pastries and regarded me with green eyes that suddenly seemed as sharp and piercing as knives. If I thought the anxiety and tension radiating off of my guests was bad earlier, it had significantly increased, literally making it hard to breathe. Fear and agitation formed knots in my stomach, and the fact that Chase's grip on my hips was close to bruising didn't help either.

"I'm sorry, that was rude," I started to say, hoping the queen would accept my apology as I prepared to blame my short temper on hormones and was surprised when she waved her hand dismissively.

"I did show up unannounced after all, and I was ravenous. Traveling through a portal has that effect on me, and those treats were too delectable to ignore. Now, where was I?" Chase had told me before that while the queen could be ruthless, she also was easily distracted. I could see that now. She ran her hands over her lap, smoothing the satiny material of her gown. In the sunlight, it shimmered like it was spun with gold and silver, and it probably was. "Yes. Your daughter. Chanell is what you're naming her, correct?"

Both Chase and I nodded.

"I had a vision about Chanell. Upon her Awakening, she's going to play a pivotal role between our two realms."

"Awakening? Realms? Who the hell is this woman and what is she talking about?" I heard Amanda Davis whisper, and her questions brought my awareness back to the humans in the audience. This shitshow was going to require a witch-load of memory manipulation. I'd worry about that later and turned my attention back to the queen and what the fates had in store for my daughter who had yet to be born. Chase hugged me closer, and I leaned against his broad chest, needing the comfort and strength just his presence alone provided.

"The vision was hazy, meaning other factors are at play that could change the outcome, but what I saw was definitive enough for me to share with you."

"Is this a warning?" Chase asked, and I was thankful he was able to form words, since mine seemed to be lodged in my dry throat.

"Not necessarily. As you know, a civil war had been brewing in Faerie, but that's not new. The balance and truce between the Seelie and Unseelie has always been delicate. Skirmishes, battles, some aggressions larger than others, have been breaking out for eons. Far longer than my three thousand years."

"If it's not a warning, why bring up war?" My voice was rough, edged with fear as I managed to choke out my question.

"I was alluding to the truce—to balance. Your husband has helped establish a strong alliance between your town and Faerie. What I've seen regarding your daughter is an expansion of this— not so local, but a larger alliance, national and perhaps global. That part was unclear. What was clear is that in the years to come, as science and technology advances on Earth, the existence of other realms won't be cloaked in shadows as they are now. A new age is approaching, and Chanell will certainly be a part of it."

I sat in silence, digesting her words. Change was coming, but wasn't it always? What she revealed wasn't horrible either—not like a doomsday prophecy or anything.

"Why are you telling us?" I was increasingly aware of my guests, who all seemed to be leaning forward as if hanging on every word. Someone had hushed up Amanda from asking her whispered questions as she sat in wide-eyed silence. Her slack-jawed expression would have been comical if everything else wasn't so serious.

"Balance. Within us all resides darkness and light. Some favor one over the other. We fae are the perfect example. Seelie and Unseelie. I encourage you to raise your daughter so she appreciates both, but favors the light. If darkness calls to her and she listens, well, that could change the outcome significantly."

With that statement, the queen stood and beckoned for Chase to join her. He gave me one more kiss before getting up, gently placing me down in the seat.

"Are you okay with me leaving?" he asked, his bright blue eyes staring into mine like he was trying to read my mind. I palmed his cheek with my hand and nodded. "Okay, I'll be home for dinner, love, and we'll discuss this then," he said, placing a kiss on my belly before walking to the queen's side. My mom placed a hand on my shoulder and gave it a reassuring squeeze.

"Thank you for the tea and congratulations on your daughter. Be well, Willow." With a wave of her hand, the queen opened a portal. My ears popped with the pressure change, and just as quickly as she had arrived, she disappeared, returning to her realm.

As soon as the Seelie queen was gone, my party erupted into chaos. Saundra Beaumont and Mathilde Augustine took point in organizing the witches. They were in damage control mode and corralled the humans into a corner where the hedge boxed them in. The only human not included was Mayor Barbie Stuart. She was human, although it was rumored she had giant DNA in her genes, but she was also from one of the Old Families and sat on the Court of the Sun and the Moon. So she was kept in the loop of all things going on.

Having the Seelie Queen show up unannounced at the town's country club? That was kind of a big deal.

The witches of the Luna Coven included Harlow and her sister Taylor, who was one of Paisley's best friends. I watched as the Augustine sisters whirled into action to cast memory spells, altering the human's recollections of today's party. A wave of sadness washed over me knowing the shower, or sprinkle, had been tainted by the queen's visit. Not just the ambiguous and slightly foreboding vision she had about Chanell, but that minds had to be tampered with.

Arabella's cries erupted and rose above the chorus of voices from the guests. My eyes scanned the crowded patio area, seeking out my daughter to access the level of crisis I'd be dealing with. It could range from a scraped knee to a fight over a toy. I really hoped it wasn't anything more serious. The day had been eventful enough. When Paisley moved through the guests, heading in my direction, she was holding Ara in her arms, and my daughter's plump, rosy cheeks glistened with fresh tears. I rushed toward my cousin.

"What's wrong, baby?" I cooed and lifted her into my arms. At almost five years old, Ara was getting too big for me to carry, but the instinct to cradle her close was riding me hard. I immediately sensed fear and confusion from my daughter, not any physical pain.

"Is my sister okay?" she asked and sniffed back tears as she placed a tiny hand on my belly. "That princess wasn't very nice." Her lower lip stuck out in a pout.

"Your sister is fine." As if to emphasize my point, Chanell kicked, and the ripples moved almost directly underneath Ara's hand, causing her golden eyes to widen with delight. Her fear began to dissipate the longer I held her.

"Be good, sissy," she whispered to my belly, and my heart melted at the love Ara already had for her sister.

Guests started to leave soon after the memory manipulations were completed. Apparently, I wasn't the only one who found the queen's visit a bit of a buzzkill. As I was sorting through the gifts and condensing bags, Lana Veris approached me. She was a regular at Coffee Haven, and we had become more than acquaintances over the past couple of years. When Lana first inherited the role of Oracle of Delphi after her grandmother passed away, she had a vision of Aster and Reeve's nephew dying and Lana's guardian, Damen, saved his life. I turned to look at her, and I could tell she had something on her mind by the pensive expression she wore.

"You're not just here to say goodbye, are you?" I asked her.

"Not exactly." She chewed on her bottom lip briefly before continuing. "What the queen said, she's right. When I first came into my powers, both Hades and the Fates visited me and informed me about the importance of balance. Where there's life, there's death, and where there's lightness, there's also darkness. Hades himself said 'we can't have a beginning without something ending.' Right now, Chanell's life is just beginning."

"Are you able to see Chanell's future?" I asked.

Lana looked away guiltily then sighed and made eye contact with me again. She reached out and took my right hand in her gloved one. At first, I thought it was strange that she wore gloves year-round until she explained over a latte that she was a touch oracle and any skin-on-skin contact triggered her gift.

"Unfortunately, I can't unless she's on my list of petitioners. I am bound by certain laws, and I really don't want to anger the gods. Last time, when I interfered with Aster's nephew's fate, Hades showed up in the bedroom when Damen was taking me to Poundtown. I don't want to go through that again. Wait, I mean the Hades thing, not the Poundtown thing." She gave me a grin, and her blue eyes sparkled at the memory. "If you want me to do a reading, once Chanell is born, petition on her behalf to get her on the list. I have to warn you, the list of petitioners is already years long. As in longer than a drug store receipt kinda long."

I sighed and rubbed my belly, taking in the information. It was something to consider at least.

Lana squeezed my hand before releasing it. "I know you're worried, but you shouldn't be. Your daughter is surrounded by so much love already. I don't need my visions to tell me how much that little peanut is utterly adored and has a beautiful childhood in front of her. Your love is her light, and her light is your love."

Lana was right. Beyond my family and friends, Chanell would have the support of the entire Havenwood Falls supernatural community. She'd have love and guidance in spades. She was expected to arrive in May, which made her a spring baby, symbolic of renewal and growth. If she was anything like her sister, who literally radiated light, any dark and nefarious forces that tried to influence her would be facing an almost insurmountable challenge.

Lana also made me realize that I couldn't control everything, especially fate. Chase and I had to take advantage of each day.

Later that evening, I was back at home. When we found out our family was growing, Chase and I moved into a four-bedroom home in Creekwood Estates, just a few blocks away from the country club. Arabella was passed out in her room, exhausted after the long day, and I was in the nursery, putting away the new clothes and other items from the shower, when Chase arrived. He was late, which wasn't a surprise. Time passed differently in Faerie, and it wasn't like he could send a text saying he was delayed, since cell phones didn't work between realms.

I heard him go through his usual routine of taking off his boots and the familiar scrape of his sword being set in its stand.

His footsteps grew louder as he came down the hall, seeking me out.

"There you are, love." He stepped up behind me and wrapped his arms around me, cradling my belly. "I'm sorry to be returning home so late. Aye, what a day." He placed a kiss on my neck before resting his chin on my shoulder. We stood there together enjoying the peace of the moment, just the two of us. A small lamp on the nightstand beside the crib provided the only light, which cast an unobtrusive, soft glow. "I'm sorry about the queen's unexpected visit. She sprung it on me, and I had no idea what she planned to say. Are you okay?"

I nodded then pressed my head against his, leaning back against his broad chest. "It was certainly a surprise. I thought Saundra and Mathilde were going to have strokes when the portal opened."

"Aye. I'm going to have to make some reparations with the Court for that move, I'm sure. I'll have to slip a case of Faerie mead to your great grand da. That should soften the old goat up."

I chuckled at the use of that nickname. Only Chase got away with calling Elsmed an old goat. Those two had developed a special bond long before Chase and I started dating.

"Seriously, are you okay? What her majesty said wasn't bad per se, but it wasn't easy to hear our daughter is going to have to be burdened with a lot of responsibility when she's older."

I turned to face him and looped my arms around his neck, peering up at his bright blue eyes that shone with the brilliance of a million stars. His blond hair, usually pulled back in a manbun, hung loose and draped across his shoulders.

"I was scared at first and worried, but I've had a chance to process everything. Plus, Lana approached me after the shower and added some perspective."

"Oh, aye? And what is that, love?" He tucked me closer, so I was flush with his body—well, as close as possible with the baby bump. His hands trailed up and down my back, soothing my aching muscles, as I filled him in on the conversation I had with Lana.

"Aye, I agree. We'll provide Chanell with a strong foundation, and if she's anything like her mother . . . " Chase paused to give me a soft kiss. "Well, she'll be a force to be reckoned with and not only smart, but kind and beautiful too."

"Flatterer," I teased and curled my fingers in his hair, drawing him in for another kiss that sent pulses of want and need through my entire body. He pulled me closer and deepened the kiss. We stayed together like that for minutes, and when we separated, I rested my head against his chest and listened to his heartbeat slow down from a rapid pace. We were going to be okay. Our daughters were going to be okay, and no matter what fate had in store for us, we would get through it together—our family and the town. While every mortal's life had an ending, it also had a beginning, and Chanell's life had yet to begin, so we would focus on the now and not worry about the future.

ENCHANTED BY MOONLIGHT - PART I

KALLIE ROSS & MORGAN WYLIE

CHAPTER 1

MARCH 20, 2022

Jasmine,

I imagine you're scared. I'm writing this letter to you . . . from you. You read that right. Magic is real, and you've been cursed. You, and the guys with you, are cursed to lose your memory every year at the same time. I (you) have spent the last year trying to find a way to keep your memory from being wiped on the Spring Equinox. Again. If you're reading this, I failed. Kage and Wyatt are going to be feeling the same way you do. If you're waking up like I did after the last Spring Equinox, you're in a strange motel room with lots of questions. Who are these guys? Can I trust them? Why is my arm covered in tattoos? What is this power I feel at my core? And why is the most beautiful flower next to me wilting now the sun is up? Your magic can grow night blooms!

Kage (the dark-haired, angsty guy) will be less inclined to adventure out into town. He's protective, but he means well. His power moves shadows and complements my own power. Wyatt (the silver-haired, assertive guy) will insist on calling the shots. He's a little flirty, but he has a knack for keeping us out of trouble.

*Wyatt's magic is inked into the markings on your arm; they
protect, strengthen, and so much more. He also describes seeing
glimpses of the future.*

Good Luck!

- Jasmine

P.S. Check the nightstand.

$\mathcal{I}$t was almost a month since they awoke and found the
letter. A few days after that, they met an elderly
woman named Ruby Howe who fawned over Jasmine's blooms,
and by the time the conversation was over, she'd hired Jasmine to
decorate for her town's annual Flower Ball and Festival. She'd
also said she might be able to help them break their memory
curse. She had somehow figured out the blooms were magical,
and Wyatt had gotten some supernatural vibes off her. Only
problem was, she couldn't get them into her town until April
14th. They were instructed to be at the Durango McDonald's
after sunset that Thursday night. Ruby would pick them up at
the bus stop.

Jasmine had a good feeling about Ruby.

Now, pacing under golden arches in the parking lot, Jasmine
tried to shove down any hope or expectation of finding a spell to
break the curse she was under with Kage and Wyatt. Her hand
slid out of her pocket, and the edge of one of her tattoo-like
markings caught her eye, a visual reminder of their curse. Ever
since she and her friends had lost their memories a few weeks
ago, she noticed something new about her markings each time
she studied the black ink. The design curled along her wrist,
faded and old.

Both Kage and Wyatt were marked in a similar way. Kage
had tattoos most like hers, while Wyatt wore the least amount of
ink. They'd discovered the meaning of some after Wyatt explored
by using his power on himself, but other meanings were lost to

the memory curse. With his left hand, Wyatt had gripped his own right shoulder, imbuing power, and he bound a symbol of strength to his skin. Jasmine's jaw had dropped, along with the pen in her hand. It rolled under the nightstand, and with no effort, Wyatt lifted the nightstand for her to retrieve the writing implement. Looking from the pen to her own markings, Jasmine had wondered if all of her ink was created by magic, or if some of the designs were added traditionally.

Wyatt explained how he focused his mind on what he needed, and the magic felt cool as it formed the tattoo on his skin. Jasmine asked him to try to translate her markings, and when he offered to read them with his hands, Kage quickly offered to let Wyatt read his tattoos. After a few minutes of awkward silence, Wyatt described the intent or meaning of some of the markings. Then he explained that there were others he didn't recognize. There was so much they didn't understand about their powers.

The light of the moon touched Jasmine's fingertips as she reached for the pole donning the bus sign behind the McDonald's. A moonflower vine sprung from the small patch of earth at its base and grew upward, reaching her hand in a matter of seconds. The white blooms never failed to be beautiful, and since her magic was amplified by the expanding moon, the blooms were twice their normal size. The full moon was only a few days away, and it felt like Jasmine's connection to the moon controlled her more than the other way around.

"Someone will notice that," Kage whispered. His body stood close behind hers, protectively radiating his own magic over them. He stood a head taller than Jasmine, his hair and eyes as dark as the sky on a moonless night.

"It will be gone by morning." A car bypassed the empty drive thru lane and pulled into a parking space next to the dumpster. "Maybe Ruby sent them, and they're here to pick us up." Jasmine nodded in the direction of the young couple who were clearly in a deep conversation in the old blue Subaru.

Wyatt turned and took a few steps in the strangers' direction and said, "I think they could be here for us. I feel magic."

Kage shook his head and pulled away, his magic stretching to move with him, but never leaving Jasmine or Wyatt. "We're supposed to be picked up by an elderly woman who sells herbs for a living. Even if this lady is magical, we need to keep a low profile. That means no luxuriously scented moonflowers the size of dinner plates."

"They will wilt in the morning sunlight," Jasmine replied as she turned to face Kage. Wyatt moved to stand between them and lingered. The layer of Kage's mystical shadow helped to muffle the call the moon had over Jasmine, and he knew it. So, as awkward as it was, he wouldn't move too far from her.

"She's right, no one will notice," Wyatt said as he crossed his arms over his chest. He had made a habit of taking Jasmine's side, even when there weren't sides to take. His long silver hair had been pulled back into a knot at the back of his neck.

Jasmine twisted the ends of her own long strands of silvery hair, wishing she'd thought to pull it back. "I just wanted to listen in on their rendezvous," she explained. "They might say something about this mysterious small town we're being escorted to that could be useful."

"They probably snuck out on a school night and hope to spend the evening canoodling," Kage grumbled.

Jasmine let out a burst of laughter. With a long swift step around Wyatt and toward her, Kage's hand quickly covered her mouth.

"Canoodling?" she asked from under his palm. He slowly released her lips and leaned to the side to look past her. Jasmine whispered, "You sound like you're a hundred years old."

"For all we know, you could be three thousand years old," Kage said with a knowing grin. They had a suspicion they were each ancient, but they didn't know for sure. Jasmine hoped Ruby Howe—the elderly woman they were supposed to meet—would help them find some answers.

Wyatt leaned in between Kage and Jasmine and whispered, "I think they heard you."

"Crap." Jasmine turned to face the guys.

She recalled when the three of them had woken up one day, almost a month ago, and none of them had a clue who they were. Well, they had clues, letters and tattoos on their bodies, but nothing indicating their age. Then, the sun set on that first day of Spring. That night, the moon shone over them, and a plant grew and bloomed in front of their very eyes. Jasmine had magically called it to exist. She may not have known how old she was or where she had come from, but she had recalled the name of the fragrant white buds she'd grown that night. Jasmine. Everything she grew bloomed under the moonlight. The same moonlight Kage had the power to shadow them from. The same moonlight Wyatt could use to see glimpses of their future.

"They're moving toward us." Kage turned and began to walk away from the strangers. Wyatt followed him, but Jasmine's curiosity kept her feet planted. Kage's magical shadow stretched thin the farther he moved away.

"Hey, stop!" the woman hollered in their direction. "Jasmine, Kage, Wyatt, is that you? Ruby sent me."

Jasmine took a step forward, in the woman's direction, and she could feel Kage slow down behind her. Her connection to him, magical or not, seemed unbreakable. The problem was, she had no way of knowing if it was the curse that had drawn and held them together or something else. Her letter had mentioned a memory curse, and while not remembering anything about her past was frustrating, sometimes she felt like the real curse was not knowing what kind of relationship she had with Kage and Wyatt.

"Hey!" the woman bellowed.

The woman and man beside the car were there for them, but they weren't whom she'd expected. Wyatt hadn't foreseen them instead of Ruby Howe. But even if his glimpse of the future was off, they had to see this through. Jasmine took another step.

"Slow down," Wyatt whispered, and pointed to a car parked nearby. "Let's hide behind there."

Kage mumbled something unintelligible, probably that they'd already been seen or about Wyatt's bossy tone. Wyatt had redirected the trio a couple times when life wasn't going the way he'd mystically seen. With the loss of their memories, and knowing nothing of their past, they'd followed Wyatt's glimpses of the future. Their invitation from Ruby hadn't been foreseen. She was offering them hope, and Jasmine knew they had to accept.

Ruby had seen Jasmine's blooms one evening in Colorado Springs when the elderly woman was in town with her friend Sherry at a book signing. Jasmine sold her blooms to passersby outside a fancy restaurant as a sort of side hustle. Ruby inquired about the flowers, then declared that she needed Jasmine's night blooms for her town's Flower Ball and Festival. Jasmine had told her it would be impossible, because she needed to be at the festival in person to grow the blooms. Ruby insisted they come to her hometown, enticing them with hope.

Jasmine was determined to figure out how to break the curse, and soon, or they'd forget the little progress they had made over the last month. The Spring Equinox had proved to be the trigger for their curse. Ruby just might be their only hope. It seemed the Havenwood Falls landscape had more to it than amazing hiking trails for nature enthusiasts. One of its residents was supernatural and hiding in plain sight. Jasmine hoped the town would prove to be a place made of magic, brimming with magic, and hopefully filled with magical creatures who could help them.

"Bale, would you do something to convince them?" the young woman asked as she fidgeted at one of her braids.

Bale crossed his arms over his chest defensively. "No way, Scarlet. The Court will have my head."

"There's no one out here," Scarlet assured, and took a step toward him. "We have an appointment to keep, and the same Court will be just as upset if we're late."

The shaggy-haired man reluctantly conceded with a curt nod, then he laced his fingers and popped his knuckles. Bale shook out his hands. His chest rose as he took a deep breath. Suddenly, with his eyes closed, he released his breath in smoke. The flesh on his arms rippled, and Jasmine gasped as she noticed the skin had become scaly, then again when he opened his eyes and turned his gaze in their direction. The irises glowed yellow, and the pupil was a thin slit, more reptilian looking than anything human.

Jasmine stepped out into the open, to reveal herself and get a better look. Wyatt's eyes widened as he witnessed Bale's odd, yet intimidating, power. Kage extended the shadows over them protectively, not convinced they would find the help they needed.

CHAPTER 2

The Howe's Herbal Shoppe was filled to the brim with Havenwood Falls souvenirs in the front room. Wooden shelves along one wall were crammed with T-shirts, while tabletops at the windows displayed candles and homemade bars of soap. The scent of lavender overwhelmed Jasmine when she crossed the room and passed a basket of fabric sachets. Cinnamon was the next scent she recognized, then vanilla and rosemary. The shelving went all the way up the wall and stretched across the room. Jars of scrubs and creams and oils filled a large section. An assortment of teas was also available for purchase, as well as a few different styles of teapots, teacups, and kettles.

"Grandma Ruby," Scarlet called out, leaning over a vintage register. Behind the counter a doorway stood open. "I found Jasmine, along with Kage and Wyatt, and brought them to the store like you asked. Now, explain yourself?"

"I had a feeling this was a bad idea," Kage muttered. "We should leave before this old lady gets us into trouble."

"Hush." Jasmine swatted her hand in the air toward Kage.

Scarlet placed a hand on her hip. No one could tell if she had become more impatient with her grandmother or Kage.

"Grandma Ruby is known for getting into trouble. The real question is *why* she's dragging you all into it with her?"

"I may be old, but I haven't lost my hearing," a matter-of-fact soprano voice barked from the back. As Ruby Howe appeared in the doorway, she grinned and slowly took them each in with bright, sparkling green eyes. Her red hair was shoulder-length, and she wore a flowy blue dress with a floral shawl. Her choice of outfit and the sparse silver strands were all that alluded to her real age.

"Grandma, spill," Scarlet ordered.

"Oh, darling," she began, pulling Scarlet into a hug. "You know I'm in charge of the flowers for the upcoming ball and festival. I saw Jasmine's blooms in Colorado Springs. Didn't you see my Instagram story? I went with Sherry. I knew we had to invite Jasmine to join us for the event. Of course, I had to get the Court's approval, and that reminds me . . . "

"Wait, you have an Instagram account? I can't even get a signal on this mountain to check my email once a week!" Bale, who had remained unnervingly silent on the drive into town, asked in disbelief.

"Does Mom know about this?" Scarlet pulled away from her grandmother to look her in the eyes.

"About what? The spell to boost my wi-fi?" Ruby shrugged innocently.

"I'm going to need your password," Bale blurted.

"No, Instagram. Jasmine. Kage. Wy-att." Scarlet spoke slowly as she went through each of their names.

"Probably not, darling," Ruby admitted. But quickly reasoned, "It's not like I left town. Again."

"No, you asked Bale and me to go for you," Scarlet retorted.

"Thank you, by the way." Ruby smiled and patted Bale on the chest before turning and walking behind the counter. "When you see Jasmine's night blooms, you'll understand." Mrs. Ruby Howe handed Bale a sticky note with a scribbled word, then waved at them all to follow her.

"My mom is going to kill us," Scarlet groaned as she locked an arm around Bale's and motioned for their guests to move farther into the shop.

The scent of earth and smoke thickened as they moved into a room devoted to more mystical endeavors. The walls were lined with dark wooden shelves, each filled with jars of different sizes. The contents varied: powders, dried leaves, roots, feathers, and oils. A large oak table stood on four legs at the center of the room.

Ruby immediately started rearranging a stack of books and journals. She shoved all but one to the center of the table. They clattered into a bowl and knocked over a half empty bottle of spring water. "I will do my best to answer one of your questions, at the very least."

"When Mom gets back from Lake Tahoe, you'd better have more than one answer. And you know the Court will want answers as early as the morning. We can't hide three supernaturals until the festival," Scarlet said as she waved her hands in their direction.

Ruby clucked her tongue and shook her head. "Oh, honey, I've already settled the matter with Lilith Blackstone, who's hosting the Flower Ball this year at the Stone Falls Winery. She let the other Court members know I invited a special guest to help with the decor, along with her crew. It's why they couldn't come sooner. But I know we need to have them register with the Court of the Sun and the Moon, so I'll ask you to take them after I show you something. Jasmine, dear, will you grow one of your night blooms for Scarlet?"

Jasmine looked from Ruby to Kage, who shrugged, then over to Wyatt, who let out an exasperated breath as he rested his forehead in his hand. "Um, okay, but I need some soil, Mrs. Howe."

"Please, everyone calls me Ruby," she said before she bent over, disappearing from their sight. "I believe I mentioned that last month," Ruby mumbled as she rummaged through a stack of pots and pans shoved under the table. She straightened up slowly, one hand bracing her back and the other gripping a clay pot. The soil inside was dry, but Ruby had already noticed. She leaned over the top of the table in an effort to reach the water bottle lying on its side. She grunted in the most feminine way. The bottle was just out of reach.

"I got it," Bale conceded, and his lean tall build successfully picked up the bottle and slid it to stand next to the flowerpot. Wyatt had been closer, but he was mesmerized by the supplies and ingredients stored in the Howe's back room.

With a wink and a twist of the cap, Ruby poured the water to saturate the soil.

Jasmine held a hand in the air, and said, "That's enough."

The sleeves of her jacket felt thick and heavy, so she shrugged out of the quilted fabric, and before she could drop it to the floor, Kage caught it with supernatural speed.

"Interesting tattoos," Bale commented on the sleeve of markings that had been revealed along Jasmine's left arm. "And nice moves," he said as he nodded to Kage.

"Thanks," Jasmine said, unsure if it was a compliment or merely an observation. "If you want to see the blooms the way I grew them for the florist in Colorado Springs, we'll need to go outside."

"That's the back door," Scarlet offered, "and it leads to the back parking lot."

"Wait." Kage grabbed Jasmine's elbow. "Are you sure you can trust them?"

Jasmine shrugged away from him, and answered, "No." She looked at Ruby, Scarlet, and Bale. "Of course, I'm not sure about trusting them, yet. But I'm hopeful they will help us."

Kage opened the door Scarlet had referred to without a word. He wanted to break the curse as badly as Jasmine, but he constantly felt compelled to protect her. Jasmine picked up the pot and marched out the door into the darkness. The hair on her arms stood straight up in response to the drastic temperature drop in the cold night air. She peered up at the sky and wished it wasn't so overcast. The clouds had a way of making the evening even darker. She would have to ask Kage to help her. He'd revealed his ability to move faster than the average human, but his ability to manipulate moonlight was special. Jasmine had never heard of a superhero or supernatural character who could do what Kage did.

There wasn't a spell to be cast or a wand to wave. Jasmine merely desired for the night blooms to grow, and they did. At first, they grew slowly. She knew they would be hesitant without direct moonlight. She felt desperate to try to keep some of their secrets concealed, since the whole going-to-Havenwood-Falls-for-help-thing had been her idea.

"When the moon is not blocked by clouds, my blooms can reach the size of beach balls," she informed. "I guess you don't have many of those lying around in the mountains, so think about the size of your car's tire."

Jasmine had hoped the comparison would help Ruby to imagine her blooms' potential size. The plant growing in the middle of their circle was beginning to bud, and Jasmine concentrated on her desire for their petals to lengthen. Her brow furrowed, and her eyes focused. She had been so determined, she didn't notice the moonlight at first.

"Whoa." It was Scarlet's turn to be impressed with Jasmine and Kage.

Wyatt paced outside the circle of onlookers.

Kage had exposed his power and the moon above them. The light was a source of power for Kage, as well as Jasmine. While Kage could store its energy like a battery, they had learned Jasmine channeled its power in the moment. Her ability to become a vessel didn't make the process easy. Kage had a feeling it was harder on her, more draining. Once the energy moved through her, she was left empty. Wyatt ran back inside and returned with what was left of the bottle of water for Jasmine.

The bud bloomed, its petals iridescent white and each the

size of a sheet of notebook paper. Ruby marveled at the flower. Her fingers grazed one of its velvety green leaves. She inhaled deeply, taking in its fresh, unique scent. In all her years of attending the Flower Ball and Festival, she wished for the opportunity to decorate. This was her year, and she knew this ball would stand out as the town's finest.

"See, honey," Ruby said to Scarlet. All Scarlet could do was nod in agreement. "So, Jasmine, what do you charge for your work?"

"Well, I was hoping we could do a little bartering," Jasmine admitted. "I'll grow you as many blooms as you like, if you'll break our curse."

"You have a deal," Ruby said, and reached out a hand for Jasmine to shake. "Now, I'd like to take a few pictures of your tattoos before you register with the Court. Addie will give you a temporary tattoo, but it doesn't look like you have an aversion to needles."

"I'll take them, Grandma," Scarlet offered.

Ruby's head tilted in confusion, and she asked, "Take the pictures or take our visitors to register?"

"Both," Scarlet declared. "Then, I'll get them settled in at the inn."

"Thank you, dear," Ruby patted Scarlet's arm. She turned to face Jasmine, and said, "Welcome to Havenwood Falls."

CHAPTER 3

"*I* think she's going to do it," Jasmine said anxiously, trying to convince herself as much as Kage and Wyatt. Her coffee had been brewed to perfection, strong and extra hot. The cardboard cup kept her hands warm while they made the trek to the Howe's shop. "How did everyone sleep?"

Kage shrugged. His black hair and dark eyes gave off a mysterious vibe, but she'd learned he was not complicated, merely single-minded, focused. Kage said what he meant and if he didn't say anything, which was often, he wasn't ready to talk. Jasmine wondered what he was deliberating currently.

"I swear the beds of the Whisper Falls Inn have to be charmed," Wyatt said with a smile. He held his arm out, for Jasmine to take hold, and glanced left and right before crossing the two-lane street. "I slept like a baby."

Wyatt, on the other hand, said everything he thought. The quality made him endearing, most of the time. His lack of filter also made him annoying on occasion. Over the last several weeks, Jasmine found herself avoiding Wyatt more and seeking out the company of a quiet, brooding Kage. Only, she got the impression Kage was regularly avoiding her, at least when Wyatt was glued to her side.

"Do you think Ruby will have made any progress with the pictures Scarlet took of your arm?" Kage asked from behind Jasmine and Wyatt. "If she does, maybe I should use my power to show her the marks being shadowed by the visible ones."

"I am not sure it was a good idea to let her take the photo in the first place." Wyatt squeezed Jasmine's left arm affectionately.

"We're here for answers." Jasmine tugged her arm away from Wyatt and wrapped her fingers around her warm cup. "Whether we find out what these symbols mean, how our memory is wiped each Spring Equinox, or where we belong, I'll call it a win."

"Um, I hate to break it to you, but I get the feeling we've never belonged anywhere." Kage shook his head.

He was right, at least until now. The trio had woken up in a haze on the first day of Spring, each with a note in their pockets. Blue ink scribbled on motel notepad paper. Each of them had written to themself. Jasmine wrote to give herself clarity. There was also a tip to look in the nightstand drawer. She had retrieved a wad of cash from the nightstand.

"After all of my grandma's meddling is done, you might just find that Havenwood Falls is the place for you," Scarlet said with a knowing grin and hint of dread. She opened the shop's front door, and informed them, "Some of my friends are meeting us here. We have a couple more days of Spring Break, and Grandma said she's planning to put us to work."

Ruby stood ready at the counter as they filed inside, and asked, "Jasmine, Kage, would the two of you join me in the back room?"

"Sure," Jasmine answered with a smile. Kage followed without a word, but Jasmine felt his presence.

"I have some *meddling* to do." Ruby playfully jabbed at Scarlet and raised an eyebrow into a perfect point. "Wyatt, you can wait with Scarlet for the others. We won't be long."

Jasmine giggled to herself. She hoped she'd be in a place to have fun at Ruby's age. Not only had the family of witches endeared themselves to Jasmine with their banter in less than twelve hours, but she loved how in tune with each other they were. As much as Jasmine wanted that feeling of being connected to someone, she couldn't help but think about how it would all be erased. What good would it do if she let herself fall for Kage or confide in Wyatt?

"Can you take your jacket off again, dear?" Ruby asked as she stepped into her natural habitat. She reached for a worn, brown leather book.

Ruby unbuckled a clasp, and as the pages opened on the rustic wooden table, her pencil sketches were exposed. The designs looked familiar to Jasmine, because they were duplicates of her tattoos from the pictures Scarlet had taken. As Jasmine slowly pulled an arm out of the sleeve of her coat, she was struck by how accurate the drawings were.

"Living in Havenwood Falls, I've seen my fair share of charmed tattoos. But the two of you have the most interesting collection of matching magical tattoos I've ever seen." Ruby pointed to a few of her drawings and waved her opposite hand to draw Jasmine and Kage closer.

"Addie confirmed something we were wondering about. Last night while we were registering with the Court, she told us that they aren't traditional tattoos, but they're more like magical markings that could fade over time," Jasmine informed.

"What do you think this one does?" Kage pulled an old beat-up stool to the table and pointed to the tattoo on his bicep that matched the sketch.

The curved black teardrop on Kage's arm appeared to be the same as the sketch, but Ruby hadn't filled in her teardrop. It was as white as the paper it had been drawn on. When Jasmine traced her finger over her own tattoo, it was the same as the sketch.

"I believe those are the oldest tattoos, or markings, you both wear. The Yin and Yang is a symbol usually associated with opposites in today's culture, but in ancient cultures, two opposites like light and darkness complement each other," Ruby answered. Then she added thoughtfully, "How the two of you grow those magnificent blooms together is the perfect example."

"As much as I love the idea of understanding all of these symbols, I'd like to focus on breaking the curse that robs us of our memories during each Spring Equinox," Jasmine admitted.

Kage confessed, "She's right, Ruby. Once we break the curse, we can work out what the rest mean."

"I understand how you must feel, and I agree." Ruby patted Kage's hand. "Last night the two of you revealed your markings, but Wyatt didn't share if he had any. I asked him to stay with Scarlet because I need the two of you to tell me the truth. Is he hiding something? Does he have any of the same markings the two of you have? Or any tattoos on other parts of his body?"

Jasmine threw her hands up in the air, eyes wide, and said, "A few, I guess, but I haven't been looking for them!"

Ruby let out a burst of laughter.

Kage tried to keep a straight face, but one corner of his mouth betrayed him. "He has marks on part of his side and on his shoulder, but they are all twisted together or layered over each other. And, obviously places he can reach with his own hand, but I'm not sure I could figure out where they begin and end," he said with a shrug. "On another note, if you'll allow me, I'd like to reveal a few more marks we have."

"Of course," Ruby said, a little hesitantly.

Kage used his power to move shadows, and some of the ink on his arm faded and revealed another mark underneath. Then, his power brushed over Jasmine's arm to reveal the same design. Ruby pulled out her phone and looked to Kage for permission. He nodded his consent.

As she turned back to her sketchbook, she turned a few pages. "I'm going to work on sketching those, but I'd like to propose that you take these two pages to the library with Scarlet and her gang of friends. We have a special section you can do some research in. Make sure to delegate one or two of you to research memory curses while you're at it."

"Why don't we all research memory curses?" Jasmine asked.

Ruby handed them the two sheets ripped from her book, and said, "I believe you'll find that these tattoos are tied to your memory, or lack thereof."

Kage looked over the sheets, front and back. "What will you be up to?" he asked.

"Oh, I have a few connections here in town to call on. I probably shouldn't tell you until I'm sure, but I think you're moon faeries, all three of you. Moon fae are rare, so I could be wrong. I just keep thinking the powers you exhibit are similar to dryad or fae magic, but not the same."

Jasmine looked at Kage, considering what Ruby had said, and nodded slowly. "Moon fae . . . yes, that feels right."

"Makes sense and seems a bit obvious now that you say it out loud," Kage stated.

Jasmine and Kage walked out to the store's front room with Ruby to find a handful of new faces. Scarlet quickly listed off her friends' names. As Kage nodded at a couple guys named Tarron and Brice, Jasmine smiled and waved at two young women named Sunny and Willa. Wyatt stood near the counter with his arms folded across his chest.

"So, what's the plan?" Wyatt asked. If it hadn't been his body language and the space between them setting him apart from the others in the store, he'd look like he belonged with the group of friends.

Kage held up the sketches and answered, "Looks like we're headed to the library."

One of the guys, a blond with a lean, tall build, grumbled—Tarron, Jasmine mentally connected the name with his face, as well as his lack of enthusiasm. Before she could express that he didn't have to help, the brunette, athletic girl named Willa chimed in.

"It won't be so bad," she said, and slipped her hand into his, ready to tug him out of the shop if necessary. "And since there are so many of us, it shouldn't take too long. If you help, I'll get you a milkshake at the Burger Bar."

"Strawberry?" he asked with a puckish grin.

"Ugh, I'll get you one right now if you two will stop doing whatever . . . that is." Bale waved his hand in a circular motion in the couple's direction.

"Don't be jealous," Tarron said, and made a point to glance at Scarlet.

Scarlet's chin dropped, and her long red hair fell forward like curtains, covering her matching red cheeks. Jasmine, confused by the dynamics of the group, figured they had a past, and the tension reminded her that if they discovered a way to break the memory curse, she'd have a past of her own.

"You guys are more dramatic than a gaggle of middle school girls." Willa broke the tension as she stepped forward, releasing Tarron and taking Scarlet's hand. "Let's get to work, so we can introduce our new friends to Burger Bar."

Willa pulled Scarlet with her toward Jasmine. "Are you ready to get some answers?" Willa asked.

Jasmine nodded, and the bell at the shop's front door rang as it opened.

A woman with red hair escaping the bottom of her ivory beany backed into the space with a stack of boxes in tow. "Scarlet!" she called over her shoulder. "Can you help with . . . "

"Mom, uh, so," Scarlet stammered.

Scarlet's mother dropped her boxes in surprise, and Tarron moved faster than humanly possible to catch them. "Thank you, Tarron. Would you place those on the counter for me?"

He nodded and returned to a normal pace as he wove around the room full of people. At the commotion, Ruby stepped into the room with a panicked look on her face.

"Is everyone all right?" she asked. "I thought I heard you leaving."

"Mother," Rose said in a calm voice, and placed her hands on her hips. "What are you up to?"

"Let's get out of here," Scarlet encouraged her friends as she moved around her mother. "We'll leave Grandma to explain."

CHAPTER 4

{Howe Hotties Text Message Group}
    Mom: Get back to the shop ASAP.
    Scarlet: Yes, ma'am
    Grandma: If you found any clues, bring them with you.
    Scarlet: Yes, ma'am
    Mom: Mother, you get back to the shop too.
    Grandma: Yes, ma'am
    Mom: And will you please change the name of this group!?!

"*I*t's time to wrap up the research, folks," Scarlet whisper-shouted, and she gathered the books that had been most helpful. At the top of the stack was a book on the Tang dynasty, another on the legend of Chang'e, China's sad moon fae, and a third book about medieval Chinese spells and amulets. The others followed as she proceeded to the circulation desk and checked them out.

"I was definitely getting a fae vibe from you, Jasmine," Tarron said, as the group clambered out of the library. His blonde hair was almost as light as Jasmine's and Wyatt's hair. He explained how he'd found his place in Havenwood Falls. He was half witch and half elf. "Wyatt, have you ever tried to grow night blooms?"

Wyatt rubbed at the back of his neck and answered, "I haven't tried, but my power is different."

"I know," Tarron replied, recalling all that he had learned at the library. "I just wondered if since the female moon faeries channel light and the men channel darkness, well, if you could create a different kind of flower?" Tarron half explained his train of thought and half asked.

"He gets glimpses of the future, but his flashes have been a little off recently," Kage informed the others.

Wyatt's eyes cut over to Kage. His stride stuttered, but he kept moving and held his tongue, causing an awkward lull in the conversation. The group walked at a brisk pace. They slowed when they turned east on Augustine Ave., because of the cool wind. Spring had begun to show up in Havenwood Falls, but it was far from warm.

On Eighth Street, the locals and visitors had come out in droves for their lunch hour, walking to their favorite lunch establishments, all bundled up. Jasmine loved the idea that some of the people, if not most of them, were supernaturals like her. Although talking about being faeries or wolf shifters or dryads while crossing the town square was wrong, even if in hushed whispers. She wondered if she'd ever get used to it.

"Kage, finding out you're some kind of moon-ninja-knight, meant to protect the royal moon faeries, has to be cool," Brice said, patting him on the shoulder. "Just think, if we'd had more time for research, maybe we'd discover Jasmine and Wyatt are some kind of princess and prince of the moon."

There were a couple of "oh, yeahs" and a "so epic."

Kage grinned. "These two have definitely needed protection, but mainly from themselves. And while I'm good at hiding in the shadows, I can't imagine wielding a sword or wearing armor." He reached for the handle of the Howe's Herbal Shoppe's door, an indication he hadn't forgotten chivalry.

Wyatt paused before entering, and said, "I need a brain break and some caffeine. I'm going to run over to Coffee Haven. Do any of you want anything?"

Everyone else debated the promise of future Burger Bar milkshakes and agreed to hold off on the lattes. Wyatt looked both ways before crossing the street and blended in like one of the many townies and tourists crossing the square. Everyone moved with purpose, but the small mountain community had a way of slowing its inhabitants down.

As the rest of the group moved inside, they each quieted one-by-one as a regal, older gentleman stood near the counter.

"Good afternoon," he said, leaning against his cane. "I'm Elsmed Fairchild. I've been chatting with Ms. Howe while you've been at the library."

Jasmine and Kage weren't sure who he could be, but they felt he was somehow like them. The reverence, respect, and tinge of fear written on the others' faces was enough to convince the newcomers to follow their example.

"What did you learn?" Elsmed asked, as his magical glamour lowered. The older fae's blue eyes turned frosty, and his ears stretched into points through his white hair. His skin smoothed, and he immediately appeared taller and thinner.

Jasmine looked at Kage, both waiting for one of the others to answer. When the group stayed silent, she said, "Sir, I'm Jas . . . "

"Jasmine," he said with her, in a deep confident voice. "It's an honor to meet you, and Kage." The fae nodded deeply in their direction. "I'm a representative on the Court of the Sun and the Moon. You may relax here and release your glamour as well. You are among friends."

"Glamour?" Kage asked with the slightest tilt of his head.

"Ah, Ruby, I wonder if one of the markings you were unsure of has to do with keeping them disguised," Elsmed remarked.

Ruby, standing behind the store's counter, nodded her head and opened her leatherbound book. Her pointer finger traced over one of her sketches. "You might be onto something there."

Elsmed took a step toward the group, and the young people parted, making an aisle for him to exit. Before taking another step, or giving Jasmine a chance to ask, he said, "You're on the right track."

Jasmine's face twisted in confusion.

Elsmed's gaze fell on Jasmine, and the room grew quiet. He broke the silence and said sternly, "My gift and curse is to read thoughts. You might not have intentionally shared all of your thoughts with me, but the answers to my questions were intentional enough for me to pick up on." Elsmed explained further, "I think you are correct in believing you're moon faeries. Maybe a princess and a knight, but there's so much residual magic around you. It must be the tattoos."

"Elsmed, do you think we should work through the magic in the tattoos before attempting to break the memory curse?" Rose, Scarlet's mother, asked as she entered the room from the back of the store.

"No," he answered simply.

Jasmine leaned to the right to make eye contact with Ruby, and said, "We made a deal. You said you'd help us break the curse."

"We will," Ruby consoled. "With Elsmed's help, I think we have a solid recipe for a counter elixir."

"Thank you for your help," Jasmine said, with tears welling up in the corners of her eyes.

"Yes, thank you." Kage offered his gratitude, hoping Jasmine could take the moment to compose herself. "You have all been so generous. If there is anything we can do, please let us know."

"Ruby does have an ingredient she needs you to retrieve," Elsmed started, "and I'll leave you all to discuss it."

And Elsmed walked to the door, his glamour glimmered into action, hiding his too-pointy chin and flat nose. He went back to looking like an elderly gentleman and leaned on his cane as he took every other step. As the bell chimed, when he pushed the door open, he answered, "Eight hundred and sixty-eight."

Jasmine blinked, and Elsmed was gone, but not without answering the question she'd thought. *How old could he be?*

"Kage, Jasmine," Rose called for their attention. "The rest of us are going to gather some ingredients around town, but we need the two of you to grow a large number of your night-blooming jasmine."

"Define a *large number*," Jasmine said with a concerned frown. She wanted her memories back, but the closer they came to breaking the curse, the further away she felt like she was drifting from Kage and Wyatt.

Rose walked toward her with a kind smile and took Jasmine's hand in hers. "I'm not going to lie to you. We are working from a theory, but with Elsmed's help I believe we have a good chance of getting your memories back."

"Ahem," Ruby cleared her throat.

"Mother and Elsmed's help," Rose corrected herself. "The idea is that whoever created the curse used your magic. Jasmine, the flower, is used to draw spiritual love. Moon magic is most potent at its fullest phase. The construction of the spell and elixir had to be personal and powerful, having stolen your memories over and over again. That would mean the caster used your own magic against you."

Ruby moved around the store's counter and approached Kage, her eyes clear of any mischief. "Can you imagine someone who would have the skill and the opportunity to introduce this spell each year?"

"We woke up oblivious to our past and to each other. Anyone could introduce the magic to us every year, and we'd forget. We'd forget the magic and them. I'm curious, who would have that kind of power?" Kage asked and shoved his hands in his pockets.

Jasmine, in a show of solidarity, wrapped her arm through his, and said, "If we break this curse, we won't have to guess. We'll remember. So, how many jasmine plants do we need to grow?"

"I'd like to start with three for each of you, so nine total. Three is a number that represents strength," Ruby explained. "In an effort to abide by the Court's rules, you'll need to grow the jasmine in the forest, away from human eyes."

"Of course." Kage nodded. "Would you like us to bring the flowers back to the store once she's finished?"

"That's not necessary," Rose answered. "Elsmed has gone to ask our sheriff to pick them up when he patrols the town borders before dawn. We are hoping if the blooms are exposed to the moonlight longer, they will be more robust, increasing the power of the elixir we produce."

"Makes sense," Jasmine responded.

Ruby handed little slips of paper, some scribbled with one word and others with two, to each of the members of their research committee. As they each shoved the notes in their pockets, she began her lecture. "Each of these ingredients is crucial to the spell we're working on. Magic doesn't allow for substitutions or subpar elements. I've given you ingredients I know you can retrieve. This is serious business, magic. You know how important your role is, so don't come back here tomorrow morning empty handed."

Scarlet rocked from one foot to the other while impatiently waiting for her mother and grandmother to wrap up their magic-spiel, and blurted, "Finally, time for Burger Bar!"

CHAPTER 5

"*H*ow are you feeling?" Kage asked, standing in the moonlight. He wore his ebony hair down and unkempt. His black jeans, boots, T-shirt, and jacket made him look more like a vagabond groupie than a warrior fae.

"Feelings? Am I allowed to have those?" Jasmine joked as she moved her hand in an upward motion. The gesture didn't technically make her flowers grow faster, but neither did simply willing the growth.

Kage took a few steps around the first few blooms standing at attention under the open Colorado sky. Scarlet gave them directions to the clearing in the forest during lunch at Burger Bar. Of course, after everyone had their fill of bacon burgers, onion rings, and milkshakes, they all felt like falling into a food coma, not finding the ingredients Ruby enlisted them to retrieve.

"I'm just wondering how you're doing with all of this?" He then moved his hands in an upward motion, waving them before the plants. "The potential spell, the potential friends, the potential past."

Jasmine thought for a second, wanting to be honest but also realistic. "The key word is *potential*. I'll be the first to admit that I'm nervous about using more magic, but I'm more excited about the potential of having people in Havenwood Falls who will be around if the spell doesn't work."

"Have you ever wondered if we had it all before?" Kage asked with a shrug. "I mean, I could drive myself insane thinking too hard about our predicament. Maybe we're actually living the same year over and over, like that movie Groundhog Day. Do you remember that movie? From the motel . . . that place only had three channels." He was surprised he'd held on to such a mundane memory. Then, he continued, "Or, we could be billionaires and not even know it. What if you bought stock in Tesla ten years ago, but you forgot?"

"That would be a shame," Jasmine admitted. "But I can't let myself go there. Learning about what we are, taking steps to break this curse, and maybe remembering a Swiss bank account number is all I'm capable of handling for now." She smiled and finished her bloom.

Jasmine stepped to the left two paces and started another. The irony wasn't lost on her that Kage moved with her, like a shadow. He willed, with his magic, for anything obscuring the moonlight to move. Clouds, the shadows of nearby limbs overhead, and even pollution unseen to humans were compelled to dissipate or shift.

"I guess humor will always be our way of dealing with stress." Kage smiled back at her.

She wanted to be serious and tell him she was ready to take on one more thing: *his heart.*

She feared he wasn't ready. She also feared he wouldn't reciprocate. Jasmine chickened out, not wanting to make the next hour, let alone the next day, awkward. They had plans to meet Ruby the next afternoon to review all their tattoos one more time, before they cast the spell to break their memory curse. So, she chose to ask Kage about what they'd learned about themselves at the library. The problem was wording the question so he couldn't get away with an aloof, one-word answer. His ability to avoid sharing was so cunning, so proficient, it could have been a supernatural power.

"Speaking of investments, how much stock do you put into those books we found at the library?" she asked.

Kage rubbed his palm across his jawline in thought. Jasmine hoped he wasn't devising a plan to reroute the conversation. And just before she could reword the question, he answered, "The physical description was pretty spot on for me, but the magical portrayal seems off. I'm not sure if it's because I'm not who they think I am or if it's the curse. The one section that resonated most was my instinct to protect. I guess I want to buy in."

"Do you really think I could be some royal moon fae?" Jasmine asked, but quickly answered her own question. "There's no way. A fae princess wouldn't be happily lost in the Rocky Mountains eating onion rings and discovering that dragon shifters are real."

Kage shrugged and offered, "I guess Wyatt could be the fae princess I'm meant to protect. He's the one who avoided joining us tonight, because he didn't want to get his boots dirty."

The two laughed and slid to the left, together, halfway finished. They were only twenty-four hours away from knowing who they were, as well as remembering who they were to each other.

CHAPTER 6

*R*uby had sketched every last tattoo Jasmine and Kage had on their bodies that afternoon. Wyatt had endured the first two hours of the examination, but since his tattoos were fewer in number, he offered to grab dinner before they all went to the clearing in the forest to break the curse. The back room of Howe's Herbal Shoppe smelled like pizza sauce, licorice, and smoke.

"Do you really think this will work?" Wyatt asked Ruby.

Ruby packed a few jars of ingredients into a canvas bag, then tucked her journal inside. "Of course, it will," she answered with a nod.

Jasmine had noticed a list of ingredients inside Ruby's book and an incantation.

"How can you be so sure?" she asked. She didn't doubt Ruby's power, or even her determination. Jasmine doubted that whatever force had stolen her memories wouldn't relinquish them without a fight.

"It is Havenwood Falls, dear. This place has been protecting the supernatural longer than you've been alive. And that's saying something." Ruby winked at Kage. "The better question is, do you want to remember everything?"

"I believe I do," Kage answered quickly.

"Don't say I didn't warn you three," Ruby said as she picked up her bag and secured it over her shoulder. "The actual curse breaking won't be painful, but the weight of the memories flooding your minds could be."

Jasmine, Kage, and Wyatt fell silent as they followed Ruby out of the shop's back door. When Jasmine looked up, the clear night sky gave her a perfect view of the full moon. And, just to the north she noticed the Draco constellation, a dragon in the stars.

As if the thought of a dragon could conjure one, Scarlet pulled up in the Howe's family car with Bale in the passenger seat. Jasmine couldn't help wondering if the place and people she'd begun to feel comfortable with would feel unfamiliar after Ruby cast her spell. She wished she'd taken the time to write herself a note in case the whole thing backfired. Bale opened his door and stood.

"Ruby," he offered, and held his hand out for her.

"Always a gentleman," Ruby doted, as she took his seat. "The rest of you can pile in the back."

As Jasmine and Wyatt scooted across the backseat, Bale closed the passenger-side door. He waved at Scarlet and started to walk away. Before Kage sat down next to Jasmine in the car he called out, "You're not coming?"

"Oh, I'll be there," Bale assured him with a grin. "I wouldn't leave you hanging."

The car wound its way through town, then turned to drive on a narrow, unlit road. Kage and Jasmine had taken the route the previous night, but Wyatt impatiently began to pop his knuckles. The three of them were crammed together, leaning into each other with every curve of the road. Jasmine, annoyed, placed a hand over his. She then peered out the window to get a look at the full moon and caught the silhouette of a beast flying over the tree line.

When Scarlet pulled off the road, she drove over about fifty yards of rough terrain and stopped. "Everybody out. We've got a curse to break."

"Just in time," Rose greeted the group as she opened her mother's door for her. "The others are here and ready to get started when you are." She addressed Ruby with an air of reverence Jasmine hadn't heard before.

"Thank you, honey," Ruby replied in her usual maternal way.

"Others?" Wyatt asked as he awkwardly scooted himself out of the car.

"My dear, if you think three witches can break a curse over a thousand years old, well, I'm not sure if I should feel flattered or inadequate," Ruby said, and giggled to herself.

Rose turned to the forest and began walking with her mother at her side. With a look over her shoulder, Rose answered Wyatt. "We asked the Luna Coven for help casting the counter curse. Not everyone could join us, but we have about twenty witches ready to help tonight. Lyra Beaumont has been especially helpful."

"I don't know how we can begin to thank you all," Jasmine said, fog wisping out of her mouth in the cold air.

Ruby's pace slowed, and she turned to say, "Your beautiful night blooms will be thanks enough at next week's Flower Ball and Festival." In her excitement, she nearly skipped the rest of the way to the clearing.

Paper lanterns had been placed in a large circle, lighting the clearing. A small campfire had been lit at its center. A crowd of men and women chatted off to the side of the fire, each holding a small jar or muslin bag. Outside the circle, Jasmine noticed a few men in uniform. Tarron was talking to Elsmed Fairchild next to some others she didn't recognize.

Clap, clap.

Ruby glanced at her wristwatch after getting everyone's attention, and announced, "We have five minutes everyone. Let's begin."

Each person moved with purpose.

Jasmine and Kage watched in awe.

"Come with me," Ruby called over to them.

Jasmine met eyes with Kage, then turned in a circle expecting to find Wyatt behind them. He was nowhere to be seen.

"We can't . . . where's Wyatt?" she asked in a panic.

Everyone began to look around in confusion, and Rose became the voice of reason. "Scarlet, you go help your grandmother get the spell ready to cast. Addie, will you get everyone with ingredients in correct order? Ric, I'm going to need you to send some guys out to find Wyatt."

Her words were concise and kind. Her voice, steady and optimistic. Her instructions and requests were met with action. Then she walked over to Jasmine and Kage.

"Ric Kasun and his pack will find Wyatt, but in case it's not in time, I want to make sure the two of you still go through with this. The power of the full moon is crucial. Are you ready?"

"Yes," Kage answered.

Jasmine nodded, but she wondered if the counter curse would work without all three of them. She fell in step with Kage, following Rose toward the campfire. Each witch poured or placed their ingredient in the fire. Some of the contents sizzled, others sparked, and a few produced smoke. With each addition, a new fragrance filled the clearing.

The witches walked to their posts, filling the gaps between lanterns. With the firelight and full moon, each face could be seen clearly. Jasmine took a moment to take in each one. She wanted to remember. She hoped she'd have the chance to remember them in the coming weeks, months, and even years, so she could thank them herself. When she finished, Rose waved to a spot for her to stand. She placed Kage an arm's length away from her.

"Are you okay?" he asked her.

Before she could answer, Ruby called out, "One minute, take your places."

Someone from the woods barked, "He's here!"

Wyatt staggered into the circle over one of the lanterns. His eyes wide and his body hunched over. Kage released Jasmine's hand and walked over to him.

"Come on, man," he encouraged. "Pull it together."

Wyatt looked green upon closer inspection. "Sorry, guys, I lost my nerve and my pizza. But I'm here now."

Slowly, and softly, Ruby began her incantation. The rest of the witches joined in as Rose directed Kage and Wyatt to their places on either side of Jasmine. The full moon shone bright over them, and at its peak, Jasmine felt the height of its power.

The power of the counter curse pressed on Jasmine, as well as a mystic smoke from the fire at the center of the circle. Her knees buckled first, then Kage's, then Wyatt's. The strength of the spell wasn't agonizing, in fact, it wasn't what Jasmine had expected at all. Instead of pressure from the outside in, her memories threatened to surge from the inside out.

As the witches chanted the last line of the incantation, *murus memoria*, the spell was completed.

Jasmine exhaled and realized the spell had worked just before a floodgate of her past opened.

The last thing she felt before being overwhelmed was Kage's hand squeezing hers.

And the last thing she heard . . .

"What happened to Wyatt?"

ENCHANTED BY MOONLIGHT - PART II

MORGAN WYLIE & KALLIE ROSS

CHAPTER 1

*T*he curse was broken, and the smoke began to clear. Under the bright glow of the full moon at the height of her display for the first time since Jasmine could remember . . . she remembered. Jasmine recalled not only the last year with perfect clarity, but all the years before that began to come into focus—fuzzy at first then like a flood. The feeling, surreal and incomprehensible, rushed over her.

Kage's enduring presence was unquestionable, as he had always been and would continue to remain. Kage was not just her friend—possibly more but each year was different—but he was her guardian knight, that much she remembered so far. The library research had been correct. And the other constant in her life had been Wyatt who should be at her other side. As soon as she could stand through the onslaught of dizziness, she would fiercely hug them both. They had finally done it. They, along with their new friends, had broken their curse.

"Jasmine? Are you okay?" a young female voice asked, her tone filled with concern. Scarlet Howe. She and her family had helped them immensely.

"I think so," Jasmine croaked with a scratchy voice. She couldn't lift her head yet, but almost. "Kage? Wyatt? You good?"

"Yeah, it's . . . much to process," Kage responded, his voice taking on a more formal tone since remembering his position as her knight—which was absurd after all these years and all they'd been through but that conversation was for later.

"Wyatt?" Jasmine asked again. Normally he would have rushed to have been the first to answer her, but he'd been acting weird recently.

Finally, the pressure in her head began to subside. The information overload was still a lot to take in, but she could absorb the world around her at the same time. Jasmine glanced over to Kage to see his head lifting and eyes scanning the area for any immediate threat, as was his instinct always. But when she looked around the clearing, she didn't see Wyatt anywhere. Jasmine did, however, see Ruby, collecting jars in her canvas bag. Her granddaughter, Scarlet, along with Bale right beside her.

Everyone else who'd helped with the spell to break the curse must have already left. Jasmine wondered how much time had passed, then contemplated what they would've done without them . . . they would have forgotten. Again.

"Kage, do you see Wyatt?" Jasmine jumped up from the ground, a little too quickly, and had to reach for Kage who was instantly by her side to keep from wobbling.

"No, I do not Jas—Princess," he replied, his eyes still scanning the area beyond the campfire.

"Not now, Kage. We'll talk about all the past soon enough, but for now I am who I was earlier today and yesterday and the days before. Don't get all formal on me now. We need to find Wyatt. I feel it . . . here," she said, placing her hand over her heart, unable to find the words to explain the urgency she felt.

"Agreed." Kage nodded sharply and surveyed the area beyond them without stepping away from her.

"Did any of you see where Wyatt went?" Jasmine asked. Something wasn't right. Why wasn't Wyatt with them? They had been practically inseparable this last year—and assuming based on their tattooed histories, long before that—as they searched for a way to break their curse. Why would he disappear now?

"No, he was here when we started the spell but then we were so focused on completing the ritual properly, and everyone started to leave, that we didn't notice anything else. I'm sorry," Scarlet said, moving closer to where they stood once they had blown out the flames in the lanterns they'd needed for the circle.

"Bale? Will you check to see if the Kasuns can track and search for Wyatt, again?" she added as an afterthought. Bale nodded and quietly slipped away.

"Thank you. I can't imagine where he would have gone. Could he have been taken? No, that seems unlikely, doesn't it? What if he got sick again?" Jasmine asked more to herself as she puzzled out the strange feeling prodding at the back of her mind, telling her to pay attention to something she wasn't yet aware of.

Kage touched his fingers to the inside of her elbow, pulling her attention to him. His eyes bored into her own, willing her to come to the conclusion he must have reached moments before. "Jas . . . my fuzzy memories and my instincts are telling me Wyatt had much more to do with our curse than we knew."

Jasmine shook her head, unwilling to believe him, but once the words were said, her heart told her it couldn't be anything other than the truth. "I still believe in giving him the benefit of the doubt, you know, innocent until proven guilty. It just doesn't make sense to me. He has been a part of us from the beginning. He lost memories with us. He could have gotten disoriented during the spell and maybe is still cursed, wandering in the dark. Whatever the truth, we need to find him."

Kage watched her for a moment, his eyes full of deep thought at words he wanted to say but wouldn't yet. "Then let us find him."

"Let's go back to the shop first. He may have gone there, but it could be sort of a base to plan our search. Plus, I would really like to examine some of your tattoos again, dear, if that's all right? I'd like to see if breaking the curse did anything to change them," Ruby said sweetly, but something in her eyes told Jasmine she already had an inkling of the answer to her statement.

"Like, what kind of changes?" Jasmine asked, curious.

She waved her hand flippantly in the air. "Oh, you know, maybe alter them in some way or remove them entirely. This subject matter is a little new to me, but we do have some magical tattoo experts in town I might bring in for consultation if needed, with your permission of course. You remember Addie Beaumont. She would be one."

"Let's see what you discover first," Kage said with unease as if he too expected her to find something. Jasmine didn't like where this was going, but her eternal curiosity won out.

Back in Howe's Herbal Shoppe, the different herbs and ingredients reached Jasmine's nose in a redolence of scents, some sweet, some spicy, and all infused with the magic of nature and that of the Howe women. Jasmine could feel the pull of her own blooms she had grown the night before for Ruby's counter curse. Jasmine's blooms were unlike any other jasmine plant because of her power from the moon. She picked up on the scent of night jasmine in the room. It must have come from the residue in the mortar and pestle sitting on the table. The smell was alluring and gave her a sense of peace to face what they were about to do.

"All right, Jasmine, if you don't mind, would you show me your tattoos please?" Ruby Howe asked as she moved over to the counter and pulled out the same leatherbound book she had taken notes in previously. She kept the slips of paper with patchy memories of their histories and notes of things they'd learned about themselves or their powers tucked within the worn pages. "We'll look for any discrepancies. I have my book, so I don't forget anything." She chuckled in the way a sweet elderly grandma might. "Come, Kage. I will need you for this, as well."

Kage was instantly at the elder witch's side, prepared to do whatever she needed in order to help them. If Jasmine was honest, she knew everything Kage had done was for her. It was his duty as her knight, her protector. On his own . . . well, he wouldn't even be in this mess with her in the first place. She remembered. It was her fault he was cursed.

Sighing, feeling the weight of their situation more and more, she skirted around a display full of soaps and sachets of bath crystals over to the counter. They followed Ruby once again into the back room they were becoming more and more familiar with. Removing her coat, then the button-up pink and brown plaid shirt she wore, she revealed the thin-strapped tank underneath. Jasmine held out her arms and looked at Kage.

He used his magic to pull back the shadows and reveal all the tattoos on her arms once again from tiny ones on her finger to larger ones crawling up her shoulder. Then Kage did something surprising and took his jacket and shirt off as well, revealing not only golden skin over toned muscles but his own tattoos for Ruby to study, again. Inspecting them side-by-side, in person. It was much more interesting than reviewing a photo.

"Oh my, oh my indeed," Ruby clucked with a little bit girlish appreciation and a little bit curious witchy fascination.

"Grandma!" Scarlet chided with shock.

"Come here, child. It's just skin, as I'm sure you've seen on your Bale. I need your assistance. There are more than I realized . . . or new ones . . . so I won't be able to compare. We'll need some new notes and additions."

Scarlet swiftly moved closer. With a hint of embarrassment on her cheeks, she whispered, "He's not *my* Bale."

Standing on the opposite side of the table to help, she took the pen and notebook and prepared to write. Ruby examined Jasmine and Kage for what felt like forever but was closer to an hour. She would periodically take the notebook from Scarlet and make her own sketches then rattle off other comparisons or comments about this tattoo or that. She'd ask questions about specific ones if they remembered what they meant or if they could decipher Chinese symbols or ancient glyphs. When she finally finished, the old witch called for her daughter, Rose.

When Rose didn't answer, Ruby walked into the hallway. Jasmine imagined there must be another room.

"Where did she go?" Jasmine whispered to Scarlet while they put their shirts back on.

Scarlet shrugged and pulled her phone out of her sweater pocket. With a few swipes of her fingers, she read something then looked up. "I got a text from Bale. Nothing on Wyatt yet, sorry."

But before Jasmine could respond, Ruby came back out with a tray of ornate teacups along with a kettle and plate of cookies.

"We need a little pick-me-up, I think. Well, Rose thought we did, at least. She's going to call the sheriff while we discuss my findings," she said, placing the tray on the table at the center of the room.

"Sit, Grandma. I'll do it." Scarlet jumped in and began pouring the tea.

"What did you discover?" Kage asked while turning a round ginger cookie over in his hands.

"Several things along with more questions, I'm afraid," Ruby began. "The first being when I asked you about individual marks, you now have greater understanding and memory than you did before of what purpose each served. More of your history and ancestry coming to light is fascinating, I'm sure more for me than you. But still, it has confirmed the memory curse is indeed breaking."

"You say 'breaking' and not broken, why?" Jasmine asked.

"The way we created the spell was to be a continuous breaking down over a short period of time. If we were to break it all at once, the weight of your memories crashing upon you in one big tidal wave would have been crushing, debilitating you for some time while your brains processed it all. As it was, it took you some time to come to awareness of your surroundings and faculties. This way was safer for you, but you'll still require rest," Ruby explained. It made sense.

"And the second thing you discovered?" Kage interjected, not impolitely.

"The second being, several of your marks are fading. I believe they are related to your memories and the more solid those become here," she pointed to her head, "and here," she then pointed to her heart, "the less solid they are on your skin." Ruby took a moment and drank some of her tea while that thought settled in.

"So you're saying the more we remember or the stronger that memory becomes, our tattoos will fade away?" Jasmine couldn't help but ask with excitement. She didn't mind and actually liked some of the tattoos, but they were out of desperation and not something she would have chosen to be a permanent piece of art.

"Yes. How much time each will take is unknown, but yes, I do believe that is what is happening."

"That's a relief," Jasmine added.

"Now, on to the next bit . . . "

And then Jasmine's stomach clenched with unease. She knew better than to get her hopes up for long.

"What is it?" Kage was the one to ask.

"There are markings that were not there before . . . " She cocked her head in thought. "No, actually that didn't sound right. I believe they were hidden before, hidden under the memory curse. However, I do not understand yet what they mean." Ruby showed them the sketches she drew of the new markings on each of their backs.

"I haven't seen that one before, Jas," Kage said with a frown of concern. He wondered if Wyatt could have marked them without their knowledge.

"I don't recognize the one on your back either. It's like mine but different," Jasmine mused, studying the drawing of the strange symbol. "Do you have any ideas, Ruby? Scarlet?"

Both witches shook their heads. "We need a little time to do some research, but we will get to the bottom of this. We are the Howes after all," Ruby said with a wink.

The bell on the front door dinged, and they all rushed to the store's front room to see Bale along with a couple other guys in uniform walking cautiously inside. Rose, who had been holding the door open, quickly closed it after the last man entered. The space suddenly felt much smaller with their large frames.

"Did you find anything?" Scarlet asked, taking several steps toward Bale.

Shaking his head of black hair, he said, "Not really. We took to the sky and the ground, but all we found was this small bag of little seeds, I think. Might be nothing."

Scarlet tipped the contents into her hand and smelled. "Poppy seeds. Could be from one of the cafes." She shrugged. "Or could be used in a confusion spell."

"Where could he be?" Jasmine turned and asked Kage, who only frowned, clearly frustrated.

"All right then," Ruby interrupted. "It is late, and we could all use some sleep after the events of today. You two especially." She pointed at Kage and Jasmine. "Take some time and adjust to your memories. I know you aren't familiar with much of our town yet, but tomorrow is Easter and some of the town will be participating in various events. Feel free to join in, but also use the time to reconnect with yourselves. We can reconvene at the beginning of the week with a new perspective and hopefully more of your memories might surface that could give you clues on Wyatt or something helpful about the markings on your backs. However, call if you need anything. Off with you all."

"Thank you, Ruby," Jasmine said, squeezing her hand as she passed by.

"If you find it hard to fall asleep after the events of tonight, place these under your pillows—one each—to ward off distractions, or disturbing memories," Ruby said, handing her two little sachets. They headed out into the remainder of the night, suddenly exhausted.

CHAPTER 2

*J*asmine struggled to settle down from the night's events, making sleep elusive. Memory after memory kept popping into her mind, and then she pondered each one, reliving them in her thoughts until she finally fell asleep. Staying at the bed and breakfast was quaint and comfortable as opposed to the business of a traditional hotel. She was grateful Rose had made arrangements for them and for Ruby's sleeping sachet.

"I kept thinking maybe Wyatt would show up in the night and it would all be a bad dream . . . except for the memory curse part of it, of course," Jasmine admitted to Kage as they headed to the dining room for breakfast. It was routine for Wyatt to be up earlier than the others, and Jasmine couldn't help wondering where he was.

Having the curse broken was still a surreal revelation. Jasmine had so many questions and several matters to look into about her family and where they were from, but that would have to wait until they could understand a bit more and find Wyatt.

Kage remained silent for a moment then finally spoke. "Memories kept flooding my mind while I was trying to sleep. Did the same happen for you?"

"Yes, it was amazing and so annoying at the same time," Jasmine said with a laugh, trying to lighten the mood. "If it hadn't been for Ruby's magical help, I'm not sure I would have ever gotten to sleep." The weight of the memories coupled with worrying about Wyatt was a heavy unspoken between them for the time being.

"I'd like to walk a bit after breakfast and get more of a feel for the town. You know, without the craziness of trying to break our curse," Jasmine said as if it wasn't as big of a deal as it actually had been.

Kage watched her for a moment then nodded. "I would like that also."

They left the beautiful Victorian-style manor with the large wrap around porch and stepped into the lovely sunny spring day. As they strolled around the town square, Kage crossed his arms and studied the area.

"They are removing Easter decorations," Kage stated.

"Why? Isn't today Easter?" Jasmine asked, also noting the bustling activity of trucks hauling away decor as well as trucks arriving with signage for the Flower Festival.

"Excuse me?" Kage stopped a woman passing by. "Could you remind me what the date is?"

She smiled and offered, "Of course, it is Tuesday, April 19th."

"Thank you," Jasmine replied with a concerned smile.

"How is it possible we slept through two entire days?" Kage asked Jasmine, his brows furrowed.

"I think Ruby's little sleeping sachets were more than she let on. Sneaky witch," she said with a yawn. "We are still recovering from being flooded with a thousand years of memories. I guess we needed our beauty sleep."

They walked a while longer, away from town square and heading north toward what they discovered was a vineyard. "It's beautiful and peaceful here, Kage. Could you imagine living here?"

"We've never had a place to settle . . . It would be nice," he replied.

She inhaled the fresh spring mountain air. "It would."

"How about we grab coffee before heading to the Howe's shop?" Kage asked to avoid getting his hopes up about a life in Havenwood Falls.

Turning back toward the square, Jasmine and Kage arrived at Coffee Haven and got in line.

"I can't wait to try the blueberry scones! Ruby said they were the best in town. I think I'll get a few to take back to her and Scarlet." Jasmine paused and looked around. Something felt familiar. She couldn't help but wonder if Wyatt was nearby or might even be at the coffee shop, being the caffeine addict he was.

"How do you feel since the other night?" Kage asked, trying to act casual as he stood in line, surveying all the people coming, going, and simply sitting.

"Honestly, I feel like a huge weight has been lifted. The more memories that resurface, the more I feel like a whole person who remembers all that has made them into who they have become . . . But then I also feel confused because I thought it would be a simple thing: break the curse and get our memories back, the end! But it's not. It never is." Jasmine sighed. "I remembered more of the night we were cursed," she continued, but Kage unexpectedly jumped in.

"Hey Bale," he said as Bale and another guy were leaving. The guys grabbed each other's wrist and shook like brothers in arms might. The act was familiar to Kage, jogging a memory of being a part of a guard of knights dedicated to protecting the royal court.

"You remember Tarron. On your way to Howe's shop?" he asked, then moved in closer. "Keep your ears open. There has been some talk about strange things happening around town. We can speak more freely at the shop."

Kage nodded. "Thanks for the information. We'll be there soon."

Once they placed their to-go order, they stood off to the side to wait, and Kage turned to Jasmine. "I apologize for cutting you off. I thought it would be best to save that conversation for our walk to the shop, then I saw Bale, and it worked out."

"No apology necessary. I realized as soon as I started there were too many ears around." Jasmine pulled her long silver hair around her shoulders and added a loose braid instead of fidgeting.

Kage froze then cocked his head as if listening to something.

"What do you hear?" she whispered while straining to listen too . . . then she heard a man and a woman talking quietly at a table behind them.

"Sheriff, I need you to look into something," the woman began with hushed tones. "The portable greenhouse with the large refrigeration coolers full of the flowers for the festival this weekend . . . all the flowers are dead. Those competing in the best floral display competition are going to be so disappointed."

"Did the coolers break down?" Sheriff Kasun asked, surprised. Jasmine recognized his voice from the other night.

"That's the strange part. They were working perfectly when the volunteers went in this morning to check on them. Between us," she lowered her voice to a level impossible for humans to hear, "I felt a magical residue present, as if someone tampered with them. But I can't figure out why anyone would do that."

"All right, Ronya, I'll take the boys over there, and we'll sniff it out," the sheriff said then he got up and left, waving to the barista as he did. The woman, Ronya, went over and visited with a couple at another table before she also left.

Their order was ready. Kage grabbed it, and they headed straight out the door into the heart of Havenwood Falls town square. Once they were far enough away from others, Jasmine blurted out under her breath, "All their flowers are dead? Ruby is going to be crushed. She must know already. She's overseeing the festival this year. Maybe we can help." Jasmine paused, realizing something else . . . "That woman knew about magic."

"I recognized her from our ritual the other night. She was one of the witches," Kage added quietly.

"Did you hear the sheriff say 'sniff it out'? I wonder if it was more than a metaphor?"

"What do you mean?" Kage asked.

"I mean, maybe they're shifters or something. We saw Bale shift, so maybe they have a police squad of dragons . . . or something else entirely!" Jasmine couldn't help it. She loved the prospect of knowing about all the supernaturals co-existing together in a town. "I mean, we've seen a lot of strange things. It's entirely possible."

"It is; you're right. Another question to ask the Howes," Kage added. Jasmine could tell it chafed him to have to rely on others —especially people they barely knew. It went against his nature, but he did it for her. The action was reminiscent of an earlier time in their lives. Memories of arriving together at a foreign kingdom entered her mind; they didn't know anyone except each other, and Wyatt, and they had to rely on strangers then too. Unfortunately, it didn't go well for them then. However, Jasmine believed with all her heart this time would be different.

Just before they reached Howe's Herbal Shoppe on the square, she heard hushed arguing down an alley. Kage reached out his arm to halt their steps and keep her from turning down the alley to see what the issue was . . . because he knew her too well. Instead she enjoyed the feeling of brushing up against Kage's strong arm. She hadn't felt close to him in a long time, she realized. She still didn't have all her memories regarding their relationship. Jasmine didn't know if she and Kage were ever a couple or if she and Wyatt had gone down that road. The uncertainty was maddening. Wyatt had alluded to them having some kind of relationship at times, but if she was honest with herself, she had always felt pulled toward Kage. Her relational thoughts were interrupted by the women arguing in the alley.

"What is wrong with you? How could you have forgotten to finish the display for the festival with me last night? It's the most important part of our booth! I waited for you but had to do it on my own because you never showed up!" the first woman whisper-shouted.

"I don't know! I can't remember what happened last night. I know I was on my way to meet you, then a wind swept dust into my face . . . and that's all I remember! I woke up on the floor in my house and don't remember ANYTHING! How do you think that makes me feel?" the second woman shouted back, more loudly than the first.

Jasmine shot a confused look at Kage. "What is up with the Flower Festival in this town? There seem to be a lot of issues around it."

"Sounds like more than just *issues*." Kage pulled on the shadows to hide them but frowned when his magic seeped out as if through a miniscule crack—barely enough to shadow an insect let alone a person. His moon magic had failed him for the first time he could remember. Instead of making an issue of it, he slowly pulled Jasmine into a shadow of the building.

"Someone will notice that," Jasmine whispered, an echo of what he said to her their first night while they waited outside town, and added a wink. She was so preoccupied with what was happening in the alley she didn't notice something was amiss with his powers.

"Nice," he said with sarcasm. Though the trouble with his magic needed to be explored, it would have to wait until he was alone.

They could use their magic during the day, but as moon fae, the strength of their power had always been at night, and even greater under the full moon. But could it be different now that the curse was broken? Jasmine still had trouble remembering the full extent of her power.

"I feel like we need to find out what's going on. I can't help but think this is our fault . . . or a result of us being here. I can't shake it." The feeling wouldn't leave Jasmine alone: they were missing something.

CHAPTER 3

*W*alking into the herbal shop, Jasmine was confronted with a flurry of activity. Panicked voices rang out from all areas of the store. People they hadn't met yet rushed in and out from the backroom.

"They're *all* dead? Mom, how could they all be dead?" Rose shouted with disbelief, standing behind the counter, seemingly to get out of the way.

Ruby arrived from the back room–the room full of supplies and tools to create and enhance the magics of the universes. She carried a tray of tea and cookies as if nothing out of the ordinary was stirring, whether due to senile inconsistencies or purposeful it didn't matter. Jasmine admired her ability to remain calm in her domain as others brought the panic.

"Rose, there is more afoot than we understand and we— along with the Court—will get to the bottom of this, I am certain." Ruby placed the tea set on the counter and beckoned Kage and Jasmine over to her. "Come now, Jasmine and Kage, let us have a chat."

"Yes, Ma'am," Kage said and strode to where she stood waiting.

"We ran into Bale and Tarron on our way, and he warned us

to keep our ears open. There are some strange things happening in Havenwood Falls," Jasmine said, setting the bag of scones on the counter next to the tea set.

"The flowers for the festival have all died, but the coolers remain intact. That is strange, don't you think?" Ruby said, her eyes meeting Jasmine's over the rim of her teacup.

"We overheard the sheriff and a woman named Ronya discussing the situation at Coffee Haven. She mentioned sensing magical residue at the site. Are the Kasuns supernaturals?" Jasmine couldn't help but ask.

"Ah, yes, the Kasuns. You saw a few of his men the other night. Remember, he and his sons are helping you look for Wyatt. The woman, Ronya, is working with me for the festival. She's also a witch and was at your curse breaking ritual, though you probably wouldn't remember." Ruby took another sip.

"And the sheriff?" Kage added, noting Ruby was elusive about his status.

"He is a wolf shifter of the Kasun wolfpack along with his sons and daughter. You already met Willa, and that's her brother Kase." She pointed at a young man carrying a box from the backroom.

"Well, that explains the 'sniffing out the issue' comment he made to Ronya," Jasmine thought out loud.

"Other situations have been reported as well," Rose started hesitantly as she looked over a scratch piece of paper on the counter. "All having something to do with the flowers or the festival itself . . . memory lapses, dying flowers, missing flowers, and more."

"We overheard some people in the alley arguing about one of them not showing up to work on their booth but the one couldn't remember where she had been, as if her memory had been erased for a block of time," Kage said with a frown. He shot a glance toward Jasmine. The similarities of their situations did not go unnoticed.

The bell over the door rang as Bale, Scarlet, Tarron, and one of the guys Jasmine had seen the other night, who most definitely resembled the sheriff, entered the store.

"Ruby? We found something we're not sure matters or not, as far as evidence, but wanted to see what you thought," the sheriff's son, also in uniform, said.

"Come in, come in and show me what you found, Deputy Conall." She stood and moved their breakfast out of the way. She held out her hand to receive whatever they had found.

Conall handed her what looked like a plastic baggie with several dried leaves in it. Ruby lifted it to the light, turned it over in her hands, then attempted to separate the different particulates before opening the bag.

"I'm not sure I would open that," Bale warned. "If that is making the flowers die then . . . "

Ruby waved off Bale's warning. "Dear, I've dealt with many ingredients and many spells. If those haven't killed me thus far, I don't see it happening now."

She winked at Bale and opened the baggie. Jasmine hoped she knew what she was doing. Ruby lowered her face into the open bag and inhaled with her eyes shut. She frowned and cocked her head in thought.

"What is it, Grandma?" Scarlet asked, moving deftly around a soap stand to get closer, her long red braids swaying as she went. "Is it ingredients for a spell?"

After an agonizing long minute, Ruby's eyes popped open and found Jasmine. "Dear, would you smell this and tell me what you discover?"

Confused, as if Jasmine could decipher ingredients from a spell or any dried spices for that matter, she reached for the bag and inhaled. Although, when she closed her eyes, she was transported back to a place from her past, a place she barely remembered but was slowly coming into focus. Home. "I smell night blooms: Jasmine, Brugmansia, Datura—all incredibly fragrant, but each with differing levels of toxicity—and something else I'm not entirely familiar with . . . "

"European mistletoe—most likely from my own stores in the back room—and a bonding agent that could unite the toxins together with malicious intent, such as the blood of the creator."

"Can I touch it? I feel pulled toward it, but I'm not sure why." She opened her eyes, asking first Ruby, then the deputy who was eyeing her somewhat suspiciously.

"Jas . . . I don't know if that's a good idea," Kage warned, moving toward her as if he thought he could stop her. He knew her better than that.

"Noted, thank you, Kage. But I *need* to touch it. I feel it with my being." With their permission, she stuck her pinky in the bag. The light of the moon shot up her arm and into her mind's eye. With a sharp inhale, Jasmine couldn't believe it. She felt the source of the moon's power and the one who siphoned it. Her eyes filled with emotion and sought the peace and assuredness within the eyes of her knight, then he nodded. Jasmine found confirmation in Kage's gaze, but he wasn't surprised. It broke her heart to even consider the implications this evidence revealed and the truth of what she had been denying.

"Wyatt," Jasmine whispered, "what have you done?"

"Wyatt did this?" Scarlet asked, surprised. "Are you sure?"

Jasmine didn't want to face the disappointment she saw in Scarlet's eyes. She didn't want to acknowledge that she and Kage were the ones responsible. But they were. They had brought Wyatt to Havenwood Falls.

"Jas? What's happening?" Kage asked, concern filling his tone.

"The light of the moon . . . in my head . . . " Jasmine struggled to get the words out. She couldn't describe what she felt other than the power of the moon penetrating her mind and gently cradling her remaining locked memories before shoving them all back to the forefront of remembrance at once. Jasmine stumbled back, but Kage was there embracing her and supporting her while she faced it all. As if transported back in time, to another land, she witnessed their past.

Jasmine fled the palace and the emperor she was unwillingly betrothed to. He was a cruel and power-hungry ruler, and she did not want her kingdom of the moon fae united with one such as his. Yutu offered her a way out. She had grown up with him at her side. He was a young playmate, then a friend as they grew older. As a distant cousin, he was twelfth in line to rule the moon faeries, but he gave up any right to that claim when he chose to go with her to China to the emperor's palace. Yutu trained under the tutelage of the emperor's alchemist and potions master. When she went to him, looking for a way out of her engagement, he had offered her an elixir. He promised the potion would take her away from this place, so far she wouldn't even remember the emperor or his harsh deeds. And of course, he would take it too and be at her side the entire time.

She took the elixir. But unbeknownst to Yutu, she had offered half of her bottle to her knight, Kage. Yutu had been outraged that she shared her elixir with Kage, spouting accusations about how she had ruined his plans. He then laughed maliciously and told her not to worry, she wouldn't remember what he had done. Out loud, he reconsidered his plan; he would have to continue to reinforce their amnesia once he determined how long half a dose would last. She begged to know why Yutu would do such a thing to them. He explained that he intended to marry her for her share of the moon faerie's throne, but she wasn't supposed to bring her knight along for the ride. Kage would only be a hindrance. But Yutu swore to find a way to be rid of Kage once and for all. Jasmine had been crushed but wouldn't remember as long as he could help it.

. . .

"Jasmine?" Kage held her steady, the heat of his chest at her back and the soothing sound of his voice in her ear. She righted herself and turned to look him in the eyes.

"Yutu . . . Wyatt, he betrayed us then—a thousand years ago —and again now. He had offered to help me escape the emperor, and I thought I could trust him. He gave me an elixir to erase my memories. I can't believe I didn't see his deceit. He cursed us over and over again, Kage. I can't believe year after year, I didn't see through the lies . . . I didn't remember." Jasmine shook her head, disappointed in her own failings.

Kage leaned down into her face, their eyes level, and tucked a strand of silver hair behind her ear. "As soon as you said his name, I remembered. Yutu did this. You have only to be responsible for what we do now. And I am with you."

"As are we. There is no need for you to do this all on your own. You have friends now," Ruby said, patting Jasmine's hand in a grandmotherly fashion.

"Thank you." Jasmine looked each in the eyes as she scanned the room. "Thank you all."

"What will happen to him when he is caught?" Kage asked, now standing off to her side with his arms folded, revealing his strong biceps, the musculature of a warrior beneath his black T-shirt.

The phone rang, and Scarlet picked it up.

"He will most likely face our council for supernaturals, the Court of the Sun and the Moon," Rose explained softly while she watched her daughter talk to whoever was on the opposite end of the call out of the corner of her eye.

"I'm sorry to interrupt, Grandma, but Sheriff Kasun is asking if you and our guests could meet him tomorrow at the portable greenhouse behind Stone Falls Winery?" Scarlet asked with her hand covering the receiver of the telephone.

Ruby lifted her eyebrow in question, to which both Jasmine and Kage nodded their willingness to help. "Of course, dear. Tell him we will be there."

CHAPTER 4

The next day, Jasmine and Kage met at the Howe's shop in the early evening and followed Ruby, Scarlet, Bale, and Deputy Connall to meet the sheriff. Jasmine fidgeted with her fingers then her hair, wrapping it around her fingers, then picked at the hem of her jacket.

"Jas?" Kage said under his breath, "you okay?"

"Something's wrong with my power, Kage," she admitted quietly. "I keep trying to call forth a vine. Before you woke up, I tried to grow a plant in my room at the bed and breakfast . . . nothing happened . . . nothing." She flung her arms wide then let them fall back to her side. "Can you use yours?"

"Well, sure, I did just yesterday in the alley—no, actually, I didn't. I was going to, but it didn't work." Kage focused on something that was normally so second-nature to them, something so a part of them they didn't have to think much about it. His brows pinched, and his eyes squinted in concentration. "Curse you, Wyatt, what did you do?" he whispered with a harshness no one would want directed at them.

"So you too?"

"It appears so." Kage frowned.

"Well, that's incredibly inconvenient." Jasmine bent down and lifted a dead flower from the flower bed as they followed the group outside of the store. She gently stroked the stem flat in her hand, focusing her power—or what used to be her power—on the little bloom. Nothing happened.

"How will we help the Howes restore their flowers now?" Jasmine wondered aloud. "This is all because of us. We have to find a way."

"We have to find Wyatt," Kage stated the obvious solution.

"I agree, but we also need our powers. Ruby mentioned a couple of our tattoos that still remain on our skin. They're ones we hadn't remembered or understood. That means Wyatt must have added them." Jasmine's fists clenched at her sides, anger percolating to the edge. "How did we not see them!"

"Maybe that was part of the spell: to confuse or obscure within the art," Kage added thoughtfully while reaching for her hand. "I know this is a lot. We have to focus on one thing at a time. What is our first priority?"

Kage, always level-headed and thinking like a soldier, helped her calm down enough to think clearly. Jasmine breathed in a focused manner, using her own reflection upon the moon even in daylight to instill peace within her soul—she didn't need power to still feel her innate connection to the moon.

"I think we should stay with the Howes for now and help however we can, even without powers. I believe Wyatt will show his hand soon enough, and we need to be ready hopefully *with* our powers," Jasmine said without doubt.

"Then that is what we will do," Kage agreed.

Catching up with the group, they followed them into a large portable greenhouse set up near an outbuilding behind the Stone Falls Winery, next to rows and rows of growing grapes. Inside, the thick and warm humid air juxtaposed the chill of early spring outside. Rows of potted plants in varied stages of growth, sat on long tables. However, Jasmine noted, most of the potted plants seemed to be untouched by whatever had caused the wilting of the other flowers.

"Over here, everyone," Rose called, beckoning the group to gather near two very large clear glass-front refrigerators. Those who had arrived with the Howes joined the few others already in the room.

Jasmine didn't need to see inside the refrigerators—or even to have heard the news—she could feel the death and dying plants from within. No matter the type of fae, each had an innate connection to nature in their own way, but for those who could grow things, they could also feel when its life had left, especially en masse.

"Introductions must be made, Rose, if you please," Ruby directed from a chair set off to the side.

"Of course. These are our out-of-town guests whom you all have heard of." Rose gestured toward Jas and Kage. "Jasmine and Kage, please officially meet Sheriff Kasun of the Kasun wolf pack, Ronya Augustine and her mother-in-law Mathilde Augustine of the Luna Coven, Lilith Blackstone a witch hunter who owns the winery, and you've met her son Brice and also Sunny. Along with the others who came with us, each has volunteered their time to assist in this case-slash-tragedy for the festival but also in locating Wyatt."

"Thank you for your service to your town and being willing to help us," Jasmine started. "We have brought this trouble into your town, and we cannot tell you how sorry we are for that."

"Unknowingly," Ruby huffed and stood. "You were under a curse and did not know you brought trouble with you. At least now we have a chance to help you find the truth and right a wrong done to you both a very long time ago."

"Thank you for that," Kage said as he and Jasmine both inclined their heads to Ruby.

The older woman introduced as Mathilde Augustine moved toward Jasmine with aged grace and grandmotherly affection as she placed her hands on either side of Jasmine's face. "Blessed be, Jasmine and Kage. You are a rare treat in our town, and you are welcome here. And as Lilith and I are both members of the Court, we will petition for your voice to be heard on behalf of your Wyatt when he is found."

"Thank you."

"Now, before we get into the magical powder woowoo and track your friend, Ruby has informed us of some unknown markings you are burdened with. She showed us drawings, and after much research with our tattoo and symbol specialists, we were unable to determine an exact match," Mathilde explained.

At the unfortunate news, both Jasmine and Kage lowered their shoulders in defeat. They had hoped someone might know something to give them the upper hand with Wyatt, but also to regain that very special part of that which made them . . . special.

"Keep listening," Ruby chided. "There's more."

"There was not an exact match, because there were several matches," Ronya stepped in to add. "We believe Wyatt used several ancient symbols infused with magical properties and intentions to create unique spells."

Jasmine and Kage looked to each other then back to the witches in front of them with a hint of confusion etched on their faces, but also a glimmer of hope. "Which means . . . "

"Which means I should be able to untangle them and ultimately remove them," a twenty-something girl stated with confidence. She strode into the greenhouse with light brown hair, a nose piercing, and tattoos showing on her arms where her hoodie sleeves had been pushed up.

"And there she is now, our resident tattoo specialist, Addie Beaumont," Ronya indicated with a smile.

"Hey! Good to see you again, moon faeries. I wish it was under different circumstances," she said with a wink. Addie pulled over a metal folding chair similar to the one Ruby had just vacated along with a step stool next to one of the tables topped with plants. She sat and pulled open a toolbox of sorts and began to unfold several wrapped rolls of tools such as a tattoo gun and ink bottles of various colors onto the table.

"Hi," Jasmine said, her eyes alight with curiosity as she moved in closer. "I don't mean to be rude, but what are you doing?"

"And what did you mean you can untangle our tattoos? I thought you said they were magical markings," Kage said, reaching out to grab Jasmine's elbow before she got too close.

"They are. Addie is the best. While she has a special affinity for tattoos and the ink used to make them, it's the magical properties her expertise is in," Scarlet interjected.

"Thank you for your help, Addie," Kage said, his head dipping into a respectful nod.

"Can I go first?" Jasmine sat in the chair, removed her jacket, and whipped her silver hair around to one side of her neck. "I'm anxious to see if you can get rid of whatever is blocking our powers."

"A girl after my heart. This is going to feel different than the way Wyatt has marked you in the past. It might hurt a little, like the flower tattoo you got when you registered," Addie said honestly. "But you seem to have no fear. Let's dive in!"

Jasmine sat still while Addie studied her marks with whatever magic she possessed to do so. After a few moments, she pulled over another chair.

"Kage, would you have a seat here? I'd like to compare your marks with Jasmine's," Addie explained. Kage sat obediently and removed his shirt for Addie to see his back. "Are you sure you're not part hellhound? You're built somewhat similar."

"I assure you I am not. I am a moon faerie and royal guardian knight," he replied.

"Ah, so a warrior? There's that too." Addie turned and smiled conspiratorially at Jasmine.

"What is your diagnosis, Addie?" Mathilde interrupted.

Addie straddled her chair and beckoned both Mathilde and Ruby over to her side. "You won't be able to see what I see, but there are several different magical ink threads embedded in this one mark, as if gone over and over again reinforcing the magic and spells."

"Can you remove it?" Ruby asked hopefully.

Addie paused. "Yes. But the mark on Kage is a bit different. There is a death curse upon it if the mark is tampered with," she added gravely.

"*What?*" Jasmine whipped her head around to examine Addie's face. But Kage only steeled his demeanor and stared straight ahead.

"With the help of all the witches in here, I think we can lift the spell long enough for me to remove the mark then the curse should dissipate," Addie guessed.

"*Should?*" Jasmine was outraged. "How could Wyatt do this?"

"He never wanted me around, Jas. Yutu has always wanted you, to marry you, and to get rid of me," Kage said without feeling.

"He doesn't love me. I thought maybe he did once, but he only wants my connection to the throne and potential power," Jasmine huffed.

"Remove Jasmine's mark first. I am happy to still be her knight without my powers. But I cannot protect her if I am dead," Kage directed Addie, his expression indicating his statement was not to be questioned.

"Kage," Jasmine started softly, her tone and expression conflicted. If left to her, she would have him go first, but she knew when his mind was made up. He was a fortress of resolve. She sighed then nodded for Addie to go ahead.

"All right, here we go. Jasmine, I need you to hold very still. You may feel some pinching as the ink is pulled away, and some tingling as the magic infuses into your skin. First, I will put a poultice of hot wax infused with some ingredients over the tattoo but let me know if it's too much." Addie retrieved her tools and the small satchel that smelled of sage and other herbs and spices. She then lit a candle and mixed the ingredients in her satchel into the wax then blew out the candle and let the wax drip over Jasmine's shoulder.

Jasmine hissed at the contact but didn't cry out; the pain was tolerable. She could hear Addie whisper something as if she was speaking to the tattoo, calling it out and away from her. The slight pinch Addie mentioned was not bad accompanied with the magic making its way into her skin. Her own moon magic stirred to meet the new energy working in her benefit. Jasmine had to focus her magic not to fight it but let it work the cursed ink out of her system, so she could be whole again.

"That's it, Jasmine, don't fight it. I can feel your magic working with mine," Addie said calmingly. "Almost . . . there."

Jasmine found herself breathing methodically through the process, keeping herself calm and patient though all she wanted to do was jump up and shake her body free of the intrusions, both good and malicious. Kage grabbed her hand and gave it a little squeeze. He didn't often initiate affection unless he was concerned or having a rare sentimental moment. Jasmine squeezed back, appreciating his care.

"And we are done!" Addie was excited but winded, standing up to stretch her arms.

"How do you feel, Jasmine?" Scarlet asked from off to the side with the others, giving them space.

Jasmine stood up and shook her body out. She inhaled and closed her eyes, connecting herself with her moon. Without thought, without hindrance, the power of the moon surged through Jasmine from head to toe. Jasmine gasped in surprise. The magic was stronger than it had been in centuries. She was stronger than she'd remembered. Opening her eyes, she looked down at her hands, then over to Kage with a huge smile that reflected the glow of the moon.

"It's back. It's all back!" she said with exultation and jumped into his arms, the force causing him to grip her around the waist and spin with her. He couldn't help the chuckle that erupted from his chest.

"Kage?" she asked tentatively. "I can't live without you, but I want you to know the power of who you were, who you are, free of the curse we've lived under for too long."

Kage peered deep into Jasmine's eyes, emotion welling within her own as she could feel the depth of him there, just at the edge of freedom. He gave her a sharp nod then sat in the chair. "Addie, if you will try, I am willing."

Addie looked from Jasmine to Kage again to make sure. She called the witches over to surround Kage. "Ladies, do your magic. Create a casting circle around us and join together, uniting your magic to lift his soul temporarily from his body when I give you the word. I will work fast while you hold his soul safe from the curse. Once I've removed it, finish your spell to release him back to his body. And believe with all your being it will work," she directed with a sure tone.

The witches conducted their magic, their energy swirling around the room, creating a protective barrier around Jasmine, Kage, and Addie. Addie wasted no time and performed basically the same ritual she had with Jasmine, but her words were more forceful than coaxing, authoritative than beckoning. "Witches, be ready!"

The magical power in the room surged, and Jasmine could literally see Kage—or his spirit—dressed as an ancient moon fae warrior rise from his body and hover just above. Jasmine's heart beat in a rush, but she added her own moon magic to assist the witches. Addie breathed heavily, but stayed focused and worked with sure and steady, but quick, fingers. Jasmine could feel Addie's magic move through Kage and lift the ink out and pull it away from his body with one commanding tug. She pulled her magic back so forcefully, it knocked her off her own chair, landing her butt on the floor.

"Finish the spell!" Addie shouted, adding her own magic to join theirs.

The magic receded then there was silence.

"Kage?" Jasmine asked quietly at first. She reached over to shake him, his head now laying on his arm braced on the chair back. "Kage?" louder this time with a hint of panic in her tone.

Gasping for breath, Kage raised his head, and his eyes found Jasmine's.

"You're okay?" she asked, afraid to hope, but she couldn't help it.

In answer, he smiled and placed his hand on her cheek.

"Test your magic, Kage," Ruby suggested from the side.

Kage nodded and squared his shoulders. He reached for the power of the moon and shifted the shadows from the light entering through a small window. Breathing a sigh of relief, he turned to Addie and then the rest of the witches. "Thank you for this . . . all of you. You don't know us or owe us anything, but you have given us the greatest gift. Thank you."

Jasmine stepped up next to him, and they both slightly bowed to the group.

Sunny Blackstone took a step next to Brice, who was not only a witch hunter but also part witch, her blonde curls bouncing on her shoulders.

"Sunny? Do you have something to share with us?" Lilith asked then added for Jasmine and Kage, "Sunny has a special gift that allows her to sometimes get a vision of what might happen."

"Wyatt told us he could foresee the future too," Jasmine said with excitement at Sunny's approach, but then thought more on her words and her stature deflated. "Although, I guess that must have been a lie because he never actually lost his memory. He knew where we had been and things we had done the entire time, hadn't he? But Sunny, I'd like to hear what you see."

"Your Wyatt . . . he will find you. Grow your amazing moon garden and he will find you," Sunny said with a cheerful disposition as if they were inviting him to a tea party. Then she grabbed Brice's hand and led him out of the portable greenhouse.

Jasmine and Kage exchanged glances, uncertain how to respond. Thankfully, Lilith stepped in. "Sunny is a bit unique until you get to know her, but she has yet to be wrong."

"Then that should be our next move," Kage declared.

"I agree, but first I want to try something." Jasmine strode over to the coolers and placed her hand against the glass. She funneled the power of the moon through her and pushed it out into the flowers behind the glass. Her gift couldn't grow from scratch all flowers because her power was to grow night blooms, but she could fill one with life-force energy to bloom once more. Those flowers were coaxed back into life by the soft glow of the rising moon.

"So beautiful!" Rose said with awe. She excitedly leaned over and grasped Scarlet's arm.

"Now people can still decorate and use their flowers for their festival booths!" Scarlet added.

Jasmine wasn't finished yet. She pulled Kage over with her to one of the tables and nodded at him. Fortunately, he knew what she was asking him to do without her even needing to say it. He pulled the light from the window by pushing the shadows further away. Jasmine dug her fingers into the dirt of the first pot and gently fed the power of the moon into the plant. It began to flourish instantly. Even though not birthed by the moon faeries, she was able to instill growth and life to enhance the potted plants before her. Each responded to her gentle touch, desperate for any hint of life after the spell Wyatt set to take it away.

"The Flower Ball and Festival will go on!" Sheriff Kasun howled with excitement, high fiving the guys standing with him, including his son Connall.

"Thank you, both. Now this old lady's dream to host the Flower Festival will come to pass," Ruby said with a genuine smile.

"Post guards to this spot for tonight's rotation, son," the

sheriff instructed. "We don't want anything else to happen to these flowers."

Deputy Connall nodded in response.

Jasmine was invigorated with the power of the moon rushing through her once more. Rubbing her hands together, she said, "Kage, let's grow a garden!"

CHAPTER 5

*J*asmine and Kage followed Lilith Blackstone from the portable greenhouse to one of the cabin-like bungalows of the NamaStays Inn, on the same property as the vineyard. She had checked them in with her daughter, Macy, whom they briefly met and put in an order for food to be delivered.

"This is our most remote cabin, and you should be free to grow a garden behind it and set your trap without disturbing any other guests. As it is, there are only two other cabins occupied. Make yourselves at home. Bale and Scarlet went to collect your things from Whisper Falls Inn and should be along with it soon enough." Lilith said her goodbyes and let herself out.

Jasmine took a moment and explored the little cabin. The bungalow boasted two bedrooms with a bathroom in between, a small kitchen, and a living space with a couch and chairs in the front. Jasmine trailed her hand across the back of a chair as she took it in. "It's cozy and feels like a home. It's been so long since we've had one. I wonder if—when this is all settled—if we could stay here for a while."

"I'd like that too, but I don't want you to get your hopes up. We've inadvertently caused a lot of trouble here. They may not want us to stay," Kage said the thing she had not wanted to admit.

Bale dropped their bags off a little later, and they didn't even bother to settle in. A tray of food was brought to them by a sweet and outgoing middle-aged woman from the main inn named Letti Blackstone. They ate to renew their strength, but the weight of what they were about to do rested heavily upon them, though differently for each.

"What if it doesn't work, Kage?" Jasmine said as she returned her empty plate to the tray. Then she sighed and added, "What if it *does* work? Wyatt, I mean, Yutu deserves consequences for what he's done, but at the same time, he was always like a brother to me even when we were young." She hesitated. "I don't know if you knew this, but he and I were betrothed from birth. He grew up believing he would marry me. When the offer from the emperor came to unite his kingdom with ours, my parents felt it was most advantageous to dissolve the betrothal and give me to the emperor instead . . . as if I was some kind of trophy to pass around to the most powerful bidder," Jasmine vented, her words filled with vigor. "That is something I would change if I were ever the ruler of the moon faeries. I digress," Jasmine said on a breath, braiding her hair into a long rope down her back.

Kage moved forward and pulled Jasmine close into his chest. "Jasmine, you would make an incredible ruler if that is your choice to go back and claim the throne someday. And I did know about Wyatt and your betrothal . . . that was why deep down I never liked him or trusted him fully. Even when I couldn't remember. Something in here," he pointed to his heart, "deep down knew the truth. Plus he was always trying to get you to side with him or be alone with him. I will respect your wishes for his consequences, but I have nothing sentimental to keep him from paying the price of what he deserves."

Jasmine lowered her head to rest upon his chest and breathed in the scent of deep spices mixed with a lighter refreshing glimmer that was the moon within Kage. That, and his presence, was all the home she ever needed. Ultimately, they retired to their individual rooms and slept the rest of the night.

The next morning, Jasmine woke up rejuvenated, ready to begin their plan to finally confront Wyatt. She straightened and took a deep breath. "Today is the day."

After a little more time exploring the area around the bungalows and weaving through the rows and rows of growing grapes at the vineyard, Jasmine and Kage ate a quiet, yet pleasant lunch at the small cafe of NamaStays Inn.

"I feel the time approaching, Jas. It is finally time to end all this," Kage said confidently.

"Then it's time. I need to grow a garden before nightfall and hope Wyatt shows up. Then I can create the biggest night blooms Havenwood Falls has ever seen for the ball and festival to repay Ruby for all she's done for us."

Jasmine and Kage headed back to their bungalow. They went out the side door into a somewhat enclosed greenspace, spotted with a few shrubs and pots of flowers, but otherwise a fairly sparse back yard. Inspired once again, for the first time in hundreds of years, Jasmine wanted to create a beautiful night garden. She wanted to release her power, digging deep into the earth, rooting wondrous seeds of beautiful flowers and calling forth almost fantastical night blooms. There was a time when she had wondered why she couldn't create all kinds of flowers, but she learned to embrace who she was and her abilities as a fae of the moon. While she had the power to give life to any existing plant, her ability to create blooms in the moonlight was what made her special. Her fingers itched to touch the soil. With an almost giddy sense of glee, Jasmine ran over to the edge of the grass and fell to her knees, pushing her fingers deep into the uneven dirt.

"I'll stand guard. Work your magic, princess of the moon faeries," Kage whispered, the tone of his words holding a sense of awe and wonder at what Jasmine could do. She had always amazed him. She was the sole reason he had given up elements of his power. He surrendered his abilities to create to become a guardian knight to the royal family. Male royalty, like Yutu, kept their power to fully manipulate the moon's darkness. Yutu chose to use their beloved moon's gift to manipulate Jasmine.

"Kage! Look!" Jasmine beamed at him. She had made it all the way around the yard. Green vines and various shrubs and plants of the night variety were growing at an alarming rate to reach the height of their full potential to release their blooms by nightfall.

Kage couldn't help but laugh, her excitement contagious. "It's amazing. I can't wait to see it in full bloom. That was the fastest you have created that many plants since I can remember."

"If ever! It's unfortunate such beauty is for a negative purpose though," Jasmine said with a hint of sadness.

"Your creation, the growth of these amazing blooms could never be tainted by negativity. We will get the job done then the blooms will release their fragrance to cleanse and purify the night. We will invite the others to see it and experience the same joy you have when you create them."

Jasmine smiled and nodded in agreement. "You're right. Night is about to fall. Ruby and the others should be in their places when the time comes." Jasmine held a hand on her chest and breathed deeply. "I'm nervous, but I know this is the right thing to do. You should know, I feel *his* presence on the outskirts of town. I haven't felt his magic like this, except when we were back home, in our realm. Maybe tapping into my full power opened up being able to sense him as well."

"Then let's be ready, because it probably means he can sense you," Kage said, standing tall while absently reaching for the memory of a sword at his side that hadn't been there in a very long time. When his hand returned empty, he simply crossed his arms at his chest.

"Remember the plan. You hide and allow me to appear to be vulnerable and alone to lure Wyatt into the garden," Jasmine reiterated.

"I do not like this part of the plan, but I know you are a warrioress in your own right and can handle yourself should you need to. I will be hiding where I can see you though," Kage grumbled, then walked under the covering of the small patio and hid behind a half-wall. He called on the moon and drew the shadows to him, pushing out the light, hiding himself even further than the time of the evening typically allowed.

Jasmine moved to the center of the garden. Some of the plants were budding while others, their blooms opening, responded to the pull of the moon as darkness fell. She sat and opened herself up to the moon, meditating upon it. Jasmine felt Wyatt's approach and willed herself to remain calm, breathing in the peaceful fragrance of her night jasmine. She'd purposely grown her namesake next to her for that very purpose.

"Am I to believe you are without your guard outside in the dark?" Wyatt asked, revealing himself sitting upon the edge of a low garden rock wall.

"I have sat outside many times by myself, Wyatt," Jasmine replied. "Am I to fear you?"

"Don't you?"

"I fear what you have become but miss the boy I remember playing with as a child."

"That boy is gone. Your parents saw to that when they denied me what was rightfully mine," Wyatt said, his voice rising in volume.

"What they did was inconsiderate to you. But have you ever considered it was the best decision, at the time, for the entire moon fae realm of Esmeray?"

"You agreed with them? That emperor was vile, and marrying you off to him was only a temporary solution. They ripped my chance at the throne away from me!" he spat angrily, jumping down from his perch.

"Is that all it was ever about? You never wanted love or a relationship with me?" she asked, her own volume escalated though she remained seated on the ground.

He didn't respond. Jasmine stood to her feet and faced off with him. "What now, Yutu? Terrorize this small town one flower at a time? That seems petty, and beneath you," she taunted.

"It *is* beneath me!" he shouted, moving slowly toward her. "I am going to take you back with me to get married and take the throne from your parents or whoever sits upon it! That is what I deserve."

"I am not going back home yet, and I am certainly not marrying you. Kage and I plan to stay here for a while." She realized her mistake and purposely backpedaled, leading Wyatt closer to the bungalow.

"You and Kage? No! If I can't have you, no one else will!" he shouted and lunged toward her, with a knife ready to plunge into her heart. However, he was caught up short by one of Jasmine's vines shooting out from the ground to wrap his legs and forcibly pull him to the dirt. At the same time, Kage leapt out from his shadows, ready to protect Jasmine with whatever he could, which happened to be a long wooden shovel. Jasmine waved him off, moving closer to the struggling Wyatt on the ground. She called forth even more vines to trap him on his stomach until the Havenwood Falls authorities came to detain him.

She sat beside him. "I will testify on your behalf because you were like a brother to me, Yutu, but you do not deserve my, or anyone else's mercy."

Just then Sheriff Kasun and his sons came in and arrested Wyatt for the crimes against their town. As Wyatt was being carted away, he snarled, "It looks like you've rid yourself of my markings and the magic I'd hoped would bring us together."

Jasmine ignored his taunt and took Kage's hand before walking away.

CHAPTER 6

*F*riday afternoon of the Flower Ball, Jasmine and Kage were led into the back of the large building that stood on the north side of the town square by Sheriff Kasun. Jasmine had shared her testimony with a select few of the Court members earlier in the day. The mess Wyatt had created was technically their fault, and she expressed their responsibility.

"Sheriff? Is Wyatt all right?" Jasmine asked as the sheriff led them down a flight of stairs.

"He is. He had to stay in one of the cells for the supernaturals. It blocks out magic. It was necessary after he tried to cast a spell on one of the night clerks. Somehow, he snuck some kind of memory powder in, hidden on his person. But he's fine. You'll see in just a moment when he faces the Court," Sheriff Ric Kasun explained.

Jasmine and Kage remained quiet as they were led through double doors into a large room. They were seated near the front of what appeared to look like a modern-day court room with a dais up front with a table and a row of seats behind it, where the members of the Court must sit. Addie Beaumont sat off to the side with a notepad. She winked at them when they sat. Moments later the members of the Court of the Sun and the

Moon took their seats and an officer brought Wyatt in to stand on the dais before them.

"Yutu, also known as Wyatt, you are charged with crimes of vandalism and harassment of town members in Havenwood Falls. How do you plead?" a woman who had introduced herself as Saundra Beaumont began the hearing.

"You call that harassment? I was just having a little fun," he said with an arrogant response.

Saundra glared at him.

"We shall see who has the last laugh then. Out of respect for Jasmine, the princess of the moon fae, I allowed her to offer her opinion in regards to your crimes, being that the ones against her and her knight, Kage, far outweigh the crimes against Havenwood Falls."

Wyatt chanced a glance toward Jasmine with fear in his eyes until he saw Kage then his expression turned disdainful. Saundra Beaumont and the other members of the Court, including familiar faces such as Elsmed, Mathilde, and Lilith, stood to their feet for the declaration of judgment. "Jasmine, if you would please announce the united decision of our two courts," Saundra stated.

Jasmine nodded and stood to her feet. Her hand trembled as she did not want to make this pronouncement, but it was her duty and so she would. However, she felt a shadow caress her skin and was encouraged by Kage's presence.

"Yutu, you are hereby charged with numerous crimes against the royal family of the Esmeray Realm and another member of our race. In conjunction with your crimes against Havenwood Falls and on behalf of the moon faeries, you will be stripped of your active powers as a male moon faerie and your memories erased," Jasmine stated without feeling, in an official capacity.

"You will be banished from Havenwood Falls and returned to your kingdom as a prisoner for them to decide further your fate," Saundra Beaumont added.

"You're going to erase my memories?" Wyatt said, outraged at the idea.

Kage stood to his feet simultaneously to Jasmine shooting Wyatt an icy glare. Suddenly, Jasmine began to glow, lit with the power of the moon. "You dare question me? This is your greatest mercy. I guarantee the court of the moon faeries will not be so forgiving."

Wyatt shrunk back and reluctantly nodded, accepting his fate. And the light of the moon receded from Jasmine while Kage looked on with shock and respect. Jasmine had never allowed the full authority that was rightfully hers to embrace her as she just had. Jasmine nodded her thanks to Saundra and the rest of the Court then took her seat next to Kage.

"The witches of the Luna Coven will prepare for the memory cleansing ritual tomorrow at nightfall before the end of the festival to give them time to prepare," Saundra concluded. "Is there any further business to discuss?"

Jasmine stood once more and raised her hand, unsure how to petition the Court.

"Jasmine, go ahead," Mathilde Augustine acknowledged.

"I apologize for not knowing the proper way to do this, but I was wondering if Kage and I might stay in Havenwood Falls for a while?" she asked.

"Let us finish the dealings with this case, then the Court will deliberate the possibility of you staying on a probationary period," Lilith stated seriously, then added a small smile.

"Thank you," Jasmine said, and Saundra struck the gavel, concluding Wyatt's case. He was ushered out a back door, with barely even a glance back at Jasmine and Kage as he went.

"You were brilliant," Kage whispered in her ear as they, too, were led out into the late afternoon light.

"Thank you. I felt my power like never before. Now, I'm energized to go grow some blooms for the Flower Ball. Let's head to the winery," Jasmine said with an empowered smile.

CHAPTER 7

*T*he next evening, the Luna Coven gathered in the small space now occupied by Jasmine's night garden at the bungalows and prepared for the cleansing ritual that would serve as part of Wyatt's punishment. They all snuck away from the festival to expedite the ritual. A lot of detail went into the ritual, more than Jasmine could fully comprehend until they escorted Wyatt in. The officers sat him in a chair in the center of a protective circle of salt drawn onto the ground. The witches gathered around him, each holding a candle in one hand and a satchel of powdered ingredients in the other. Mathilde explained the ceremony; it was straightforward, simple but powerful, with no pain involved. They began a simple chant, first one voice, then followed by each witch until they recited it in chorus.

Panic flared in Wyatt's eyes, chased by genuine emotion. Jasmine felt a pang of sorrow for him but held it in check. His eyes found hers and then Kage, standing at her side. An expression of peace came upon him, and he offered a small smile.

"I was wrong. I'm sorry, Jasmine, and to you, Kage. Thank you for this mercy and for not tossing me out on my own. I'll be okay, Jazzy. Perhaps, we'll see each other again," Yutu said using his childhood nickname for her, then turned back to the witches, hypnotized by their spell.

Kage grasped ahold of Jasmine's hand and laced his fingers within hers. "He'll be all right. You did the right thing."

"I know. It's just difficult. I don't want to be callous about it, but I want to feel the feelings and then let them go. But it's still hard."

At once, the chanting stopped. The witches, everyone in unison, tipped their candle and dripped wax inside the circle then opened their satchel and blew the powdered contents directly at Wyatt, covering him from head to toe in the strange mix of ingredients. He began sneezing then suddenly opened his eyes and looked around with fear and uncertainty. The witches broke the circle and stepped back.

Jasmine felt compelled to go to him, placing her hand on his shoulder. "Hey, you're all right. Your name is Yutu, and one of these nice people is going to take you home. You were on your way back but lost your way. I know you'll find it again. Be well," she said with a lump in her throat then stepped back, allowing Sheriff Kasun to gently usher Wyatt out of her garden.

Each member of the coven greeted her as they took their leave from her bungalow. She owed them a great deal and wanted them to know she appreciated what they did for Wyatt, and for her and Kage. Finally, the women she knew were left. She hugged Mathilde Augustine and her daughter-in-law Ronya. Then embraced Scarlet, Rose, and Ruby Howe next. "I couldn't have done any of this without you all. You have helped us find who we are and freed us to continue to be us. I don't know if we can stay yet, but I hope we can continue being friends."

"Oh, dear, you can't get rid of us that easily," Ruby said with a smile as she patted Jasmine's cheek. "Your night blooms at the ball last night were stunning. Lilith and I have been receiving compliments all day."

"Plus we still have a little of the festival left to wow all the people of Havenwood Falls with your amazing night blooms!"

Scarlett said, practically jumping up and down on the balls of her feet with excitement.

Jasmine caught a look from Kage that said, *why not?* The idea of bringing forth something fresh and alive and beautiful invigorated her. Jasmine then smiled at Scarlet and said, "Lead the way!"

Even though it was only a handful of blocks to the town square, several of the witches had brought cars because the evenings were still pretty cold and they wanted to get there quickly. Jasmine and Kage piled into a car with Scarlet, Rose, Ruby, and a couple other stragglers. The town was alive and filled with an abundance of floral scents. People gathered by food trucks. Booths of not only flowers but products created with, or inspired by, flowers, as well as vendors of food and beverages, lined the grassy area of the square. Lively music played from a local band under the covered gazebo.

The Howes ushered Jasmine and Kage to a booth at the center of the festival. They had worked out a plan earlier in their stay for Jasmine to create her flowers without the human population of the town knowing it was supernaturally enhanced growth.

"Ready?" Jasmine whispered to Kage, who nodded with a smile. They snuck behind a covered janitorial booth nearby, she lowered to her knees, and dug her hands into the earth. Kage pulled shadows to cover and hide what she grew so the patrons of the festival would be none the wiser. A thin vine quickly and quietly grew, climbing sneakily up tent poles and across the tops of all the booths until the entire area was covered. She went back into the Howes' booth, where there were empty pots of dirt, and she grew a large bush of night jasmine, angel's trumpet, queen of the night, and night phlox also under the cover of Kage's shadow.

"Okay, it's all set up. Just tell me when," Jasmine mentioned covertly to Ruby who sat in a chair behind a table, selling soaps, bath bombs, and other items from Howe's Herbal Shoppe.

"Very good," Ruby said with a sneaky smile. "The festival is almost at an end. So get ready."

Jasmine reached up and gently held onto the vining Moonflower Morning Glory. Just then an announcement came over the sound system. "Thank you for attending this year's Flower Festival! The booths will be closing in fifteen minutes."

Music resumed playing for a final song, and some attendees danced in the grass.

"Now, Jasmine," Ruby said. Kage released the shadows back into the night, and Jasmine smiled and pushed the magic of her moonlight into the vine while also touching one of the pots with her opposite hand. As if flipping a switch, moonflowers along the vine burst open one by one all across the festival. Jasmine quickly touched each of the pots in the Howes' booth, and those flowers exploded into blooms as well. With an added touch of moon magic, the flowers glowed as if lit with little white lights.

"Oohs" and "ahhs" echoed around the park. The sight was otherworldly, or the elaborate plan of a garden club to any onlookers who were unaware of the supernatural around them.

"Jasmine," Ruby breathed her name with wonder and awe, extending her hand for Jasmine to take. "This is beyond what I had imagined. You have made my dream come true. Thank you."

Jasmine could only smile in return, fighting the emotion that threatened to burst from her heart. Kage grabbed her other hand and stood beside her, admiring her work as well. In a magical addition, fireworks burst from behind the town hall's clock tower, exploding with sparks of greens, blues, purples, whites, and reds throughout the sky.

"I hope it's okay that I petitioned the Court to stay on our behalf," Jasmine said to Kage, still watching the sky.

"You have gone through a lot, Jas. I would understand if you wanted a fresh start free from anything reminding you of your past," Kage said hesitantly.

She then turned to face him, to see his eyes clearly. "Kage, do you want to leave?"

After a moment of staring deep into her eyes, he said, "Jasmine, I knew my place was by your side even before I took the vows of a knight. I wanted to be the type of man you deserved to have at your side, not one who might play games with your heart. I gave up the powers bestowed on the male faeries. To answer your question, I will stay at your side as long as you want me around. So the question to you is: do you want me to stay with you?"

"Always, Kage, never question that. We have danced around the idea of *us* time and again throughout history, now that I can remember. I want you to be more than my knight. I want us to have a fresh start here in Havenwood Falls and explore who we can be free of all of our past." She took a deep breath. "I have always loved you, Kage," Jasmine confessed under the light of the moon behind them, and the muted sounds of fireworks, music, and revelry in the background.

"I love you, Jasmine," Kage replied. Together they leaned toward each other and kissed. The night jasmine blooms turned toward Jasmine and Kage, illuminating them with their magical glow.

Ruby pulled Scarlet into a hug and whispered with glee, "Truly enchanted by moonlight."

BLOSSOM

SUSAN BURDORF

CHAPTER 1

*J*udi Lowe checked the map for the third time, still confused about the directions she had for Havenwood Falls, glancing between her malfunctioning GPS and the paper directions she'd scribbled down from the map that had only been able to give her a general idea for the area where she was headed. The directions were so vague, they were worse than useless. Her eye was caught by a sign for a rest stop ahead. Pulling off the road, she drove into the large parking lot behind a tour bus with the words "Havenwood Falls or bust" scribbled on the back window. A group of people exited the bus, all of whom seemed excited and ready for an adventure.

A young girl cut in front of her in the queue for the ladies room with an apologetic shrug.

"Sorry," she said. "I really gotta go, and the bus for Havenwood Falls is about to leave."

"You're all headed to Havenwood Falls?" Judi looked around at the crowd. "So am I."

"Did I hear you say you are headed to Havenwood Falls?" said a woman at the information counter as Judi exited the bathroom and passed by the desk.

"Why yes, I am. At least, I hope I am. I have been driving around trying to find the road, but I keep missing it. I was going to ask . . . " Judi pulled the map from her pocket.

The woman behind the counter smiled in a very friendly manner. She handed the map back to Judi and nodded to the man who was standing nearby in a bus driver's uniform. The name BRAD was embroidered above the pocket.

"You'd better follow that bus," the woman advised. "That would be the easiest way to get there."

"Oh, what a great idea," Judi said as she tucked the map away in her pocket. "Thank you. Is the bus leaving soon?"

Brad wandered over, and hearing the end of the conversation, he nodded. "Yes, we're just waiting for a few stragglers then we are off. Feel free to follow us there. She's right, following us is the best way to find Havenwood Falls."

He smiled widely, and Judi couldn't help but smile back. She was suddenly less anxious, and the excitement of finding Havenwood Falls was rearing its head again. She loved the idea of a new adventure.

Within ten minutes, she was on the road headed toward her future with a lighter heart and a hope for a great retirement. Teaching science to eighth graders had been her life's work, but now she was ready to make her life work for her.

Humming to the tunes on the radio, she saw the sign welcoming visitors and residents to Havenwood Falls and felt her heart beat a little faster. Finding out her elderly aunt had left her a small house in this strangely hard to find town had been a blessing at just the right time.

Checking the address of the house she was to call home, she took a moment to observe the town as she drove around the square that appeared to be the center of town, or at least the business district. She saw a coffee shop and a gift shop with a very pretty display window filled with soaps and candles. She also noticed a music shop and a consignment shop with the most interesting items in the window. She knew she would be shopping there soon. She loved unusual and unique items. A bookstore had a sign welcoming a local author named Sherry Grimes to an event in a few weeks. She would definitely be checking out the bookstore, as reading was one of her many hobbies.

There were people everywhere, some with shopping bags and some with coffee and small bags that might have contained bagels or muffins. The town looked lively, and the residents or tourists appeared to be enjoying themselves. She felt at home here, and she'd only just arrived.

"Coffee sounds good," she thought as a parking space opened up on the street in front of a place called Coffee Haven, and on impulse, she pulled in.

Turning off the car, she exited the vehicle and stretched her cramped muscles. Growing old was no fun, but she reveled at the cool mountain air of late spring in Colorado that touched her bare skin. Her bones creaked as she walked. After being in the car for so long, her knees were a bit weak, the brief respite of walking at the travel stop not quite enough exercise to get the kinks out.

The rich smells of fresh brewed coffee, married with the scent of fresh baked blueberry scones and the aroma of melted chocolate, hit her the moment she entered Coffee Haven. Judi breathed in deeply. She felt instantly energized and happy to be there. A feeling of euphoric relief took over, bringing forth a joy she hadn't experienced in a long time.

She was home.

"Hi," said the pretty girl at the counter when it was Judi's turn to order.

"Hello, young lady," Judi responded. "I would love a black coffee . . . no, change that. I want the most exotic flavored coffee you have in the store. Don't tell me what it is. Surprise me."

The girl looked at her with a raised eyebrow and wide smile. "Are you sure?"

Judi squared her shoulders as if unloading a burden and

nodded. New life, new outlook—that was going to be her motto from now on. She was going to experiment and not be afraid of challenges. What was the sense of changing her geography if she wasn't willing to change everything else?

"Thank you," she said when the barista mixing her coffee handed her the cup. She didn't even take a whiff because she was afraid she would chicken out if she didn't like the way it smelled.

The coffee was everything she'd hoped for and more. As she rolled the liquid around in her mouth, the flavors of smoked hickory, a little fruitiness, and some nuttiness blended together in an unexpected burst of flavors that both tantalized and invigorated. All in all, a great cup of coffee and absolutely nothing she would have tried before if she hadn't decided to be daring.

Staring at the cup before taking another sip, she marveled at how her choice to make a difference in such a small way could have such delightful results.

"Are you lost?"

The voice at her back startled her, and she turned so quickly, she nearly dropped the cup. Only quick thinking by the woman who stood there smiling at her prevented caffeine disaster. As the cup slipped from her fingers, the other woman grabbed it and returned it to Judi so quickly, she was certain she'd imagined a flash of bright light that had accompanied her movements.

"Thanks," Judi said as she gripped the cup tighter. The warmth gave her courage as she stared at the intriguing woman in front of her. "My name's Judi." She extended her hand, which the other woman enfolded her in her own. She had smooth strong hands, several bracelets stacked on each wrist, and a firm handshake, which Judi appreciated.

"Addie," she answered. Her head tilted, and the light gleamed on a small stone piercing in the side of her nose. "Are you new to Havenwood Falls?" Her gaze was penetrating, but not unkind.

"I am," Judi said. Suddenly she didn't want to leave this woman's presence. "Any suggestions on what I should check out next?"

Addie rattled off several suggestions, ticking them on her fingers, each one adorned by a ring. She seemed to have the kind of knowledge of the town and the surrounding area of someone who'd lived here all her life.

People flowed around them in waves, but Judi hardly noticed them. She was feeling especially calm and contented talking to this woman whom she'd just met, and she was reassured every second they talked that coming to Havenwood Falls had been the right decision.

"Will you be staying here long?" Addie asked. She looked especially curious to hear Judi's answer.

"Yes, I am. I just retired. I was trying to decide what to do with the rest of my life when I got a letter from a lawyer about a house I had inherited from an aunt whom I had forgotten lived in Colorado. I received a flyer from the town the same day, and so, here I am!"

"Oh, who was your aunt?"

"Agatha Browning. She lived in a little cottage with a small garden. At least, that is what it looks like in the pictures I saw. I am looking forward to puttering around in her garden."

"Aw, Aggie." She frowned, her brown eyes softening. "I'm so sorry for your loss. Aggie was a sweet woman, and her vegetables were out of this world. I remember folks always talking about the size of her produce at her vegetable stand, and I remember her leaving baskets with her vegetables on the porches of people in town when I was a little girl, right up until a few years ago when getting around was a little more difficult for her. I hope her garden is still as good as it was."

"Tomatoes, and cucumbers, and I remember her zucchini were always huge! At least they looked that way in the pictures she always sent us." Judi laughed at the memory of her aunt's baseball bat-sized zucchini.

"Well, I'm sure I'll see you again soon. It's a small town. If you need anything, here's my number. I'll come check in on you, if that's okay?"

"I would love that," Judi said. And she was surprised that she really meant it. Even though Addie was obviously so much younger than her own sixty-two years, the young woman reminded her of some of her younger students when they were college-aged, as Addie looked to be in her twenties. "I hope to be able to find her place. My GPS is not working well for some reason. Maybe the mountains are interfering with the signal. As a matter of fact, coming into town I had to follow a bus with tourists on it because my GPS couldn't get me any farther than the information rest area outside town."

"Oh, yes." Addie nodded. "Something in the mountains affects it. People are always having problems with it. With phones and internet, too. Just a warning. But I know exactly where your aunt's cottage is. Straight down this road a mile or so and then just as it starts climbing the mountain, her cottage is second on the left. It's a small white one with black trim and the quintessential white picket fence around it. You will recognize it by the profusion of flowers. Your aunt loved flowers almost as much as her vegetables. So glad you were able to find us. Welcome to town. I'll see you soon." Addie's gaze was intense as she met Judi's eyes squarely, and Judi had the sensation of being sized up for some reason.

Thanking Addie for her directions, Judi said, "I hope I will see you soon. You are welcome to come to the house anytime."

And she meant the invitation. She imagined she and Addie could be good neighbors, if not good friends.

Addie nodded. Once more her gaze left Judi wondering what the woman was looking for from her. After a few more pleasantries, Addie waved a short good-bye and moved off.

Judi watched her disappear into the crowd. Sipping her coffee, Judi made her way to her car and drove in the direction her new friend had indicated.

The more she drove through the town, the more she knew Havenwood Falls was the perfect place for her retirement years. Its quaint buildings and variety of unique shops were so welcoming. She had never been anywhere before that felt so much like home.

CHAPTER 2

*P*erhaps it was remembering her aunt's few letters or perhaps it was just her new spirit of adventure, but she was excited as she drove up to the cottage she recognized the moment she saw it. Addie's description had been perfect.

Parking in front of the house, she walked forward to the gate in the fence and stopped. She sighed. The cottage was exactly as she'd hoped it would be. It was as if she'd stepped back in time. The house sat in the middle of a beautiful garden full of color and late spring blooms.

An amateur gardener herself, Judi recognized some of the wildflowers popular in Colorado at this time of the year, like the bright blooms of the fireweed, their tall stalks topped by pinkish-purple blossoms nodding a welcome to her as she opened the gate and stepped inside.

She touched the bell-like flowers of the bluebell and marveled at the pretty star-shaped blue columbine, which if she remembered correctly was the Colorado state flower. The Indian paintbrush flower was flaming in all its orange-red glory, and the delicate blanket flower was showing off its tie-dyed effect of red, orange, and yellow centers with petals like a sunflower. May was the best month for flowers in this part of the country that was for certain, judging by her aunt's garden.

The garden was rife with color, and Judi couldn't decide what to touch or where to look first. Her aunt had always loved her garden, and it was easy to see she took great care of it. No weed would ever venture forth here without fearing for its life. The garden was inlaid with grassy areas, and stone benches were set in several areas around the grouped plants for people to sit and enjoy the view and the scents of her garden.

Insects buzzed, and the faint whisper of wind chimes could be heard in the air. Garden stones were laid out, inviting visitors to follow the garden around the side and to the back of the house, so Judi did just that.

A small wooden shed sat in the back left corner, a taller fence surrounding this part of the property with strings to encourage plants to grow upward. Cute wooden signs separated the various vegetable and herb patches in an orderly fashion, making it hard to believe her aunt had died a few months ago as everything still looked so well tended.

Judi saw signs for tomato plants, zucchini, and many other varieties of vegetables set out in the larger raised beds, with the herbs in small container beds around the back patio. A table with an umbrella currently folded up and four iron chairs set out around it stood on the stone patio. Some scraggly vines crawled over mostly everything, and she decided she would have to tackle those first, once she got started on the garden. They were the only blight on the otherwise orderly garden.

"Well, Auntie, I bet you really enjoyed some wonderful cups of tea or coffee out here, and I hope to continue that tradition." She didn't expect an answer to her comment and nearly jumped out of her skin when a deep male voice spoke behind her.

"Yep, your aunt sure did enjoy her garden."

Whirling around, Judi was shocked to see a man in a very fancy suit sitting on one of the benches. He'd been in the shadows, and she'd missed seeing him as her eyes had only been for the garden, and of course, she hadn't been expecting company.

Rising from the bench, he walked toward her with an outstretched hand. "Otis Granger at your service, ma'am. You must be Miss Judi, Aggie's niece. She talked about you all the time."

Judi accepted the proffered hand, surprised to feel the rough calluses on his palms that spoke of a hard-working life, and not one of leisure that his suit and tie implied.

He might have been around her age, but it was hard to tell as his face was weathered and his hair pure white and thick. His step was spry, though, and he met her gaze with a slightly tilted smile like she amused him, and that disconcerted her a bit. He had the air of a jovial person, and she was drawn to his twinkling eyes. Her lips curled up slightly in greeting.

"I wasn't expecting company," she said, letting go of his hand with some reluctance. His hand was warm and fit nicely in hers, and she felt like she knew him even though they'd only just met. This was the second time since arriving in her new hometown that she met someone she was so comfortable with.

"I'm sure you weren't."

Judi thought that was his way of apologizing for his intrusion, but she wasn't sure. Suddenly feeling awkward, she didn't know what to do or say next.

"I'm here at your aunt's request, and I guess you need these now that you're here." He pulled out two envelopes from the inside pocket of his suit coat.

Handing her one envelope, he said, "That's the letter of ownership, the deed, to the house. It's all paid off. House, contents, and land they sit on all belong to you."

Judi accepted the extended envelope, not sure why he'd brought them to her in person, and not really sure why he had them at all.

"Oh," he said casually as if reading her mind, "I was also

your aunt's lawyer. She asked me to greet you when you arrived and show you what's what."

He held the second letter in his hand, turning it over as if considering what to do with it. Tapping it against his chin as he studied her, he seemed to be making his mind up about something.

Judi nodded to the letter he was holding onto and said, "Is that for me?"

"Y-y-yes, but I think I need to give that to you later. How about we tour the property first? There are some things you probably need to know before you decide if you're staying or not."

"Oh, I'm staying," Judi assured him, reaching for the letter, but he put it inside his jacket first. Waving his hand toward the house in a Vanna White-like gesture, he nodded toward the back door to the house.

"How about if we start with the house and then you can see the rest."

"This all sounds very mysterious . . . " Judi started to say before he waved his hand to get her attention.

"Not at all. Your aunt just wanted to be sure you fully understood your responsibilities before accepting the house and the garden."

Now it was Judi's turn to look at him with some speculation. Raising an eyebrow, she said, "I get the feeling there is something you are not telling me."

"All in due time, all in due time," he repeated himself. Nodding to the back door, he walked in front of her to turn the unlocked knob then stepped back to allow her to precede him inside.

"I have to say," Judi said looking at him over her shoulder, "I have had a very long drive, and I'm really not up to having company. I think I can find my way around the cottage and the property on my own, Mr. Granger—"

"Otis," he interrupted as he followed her inside. He moved

in front of her to the doorway leading from the mud room into the interior of the house. He had positioned himself in such a way that he was blocking her entrance into the rest of the house as he turned to face her. His expression was serious, but not unkind.

"Otis," she said, acknowledging his preferred use of his first name, "I really just need to rest."

"No worries." He brushed aside her gentle dismissal with a wide smile, revealing large white teeth and wrinkles around his bright blue eyes. "I have my orders, though. And your aunt," he lowered his voice like they were sharing secrets, "was very big on people doing what they were told."

Judi chuckled. That was definitely true. She remembered her mother telling her of the many times when in her youth she'd tried to get away with something and Agatha had found out about it. Her older sister made her confess if she needed to, or finish what she'd started the way Agatha wanted her to do it. All that had happened before Agatha had moved here to Havenwood Falls, when Judi was a young woman.

Judi had received letters of both encouragement and chastisement herself from her mother's sister over the years when she was younger. Judi had always protested—what teen doesn't think they know better? But Aunt Aggie always won out in the end. And, to be honest, she had always been right. In her later years, Judi found herself doing exactly the same to her students, the echo of her aunt's remonstrations in her mind as she did this, and she hoped her students had known she'd only had their best interests at heart too.

Thinking about the students she'd taught over the years brought a smile to her lips and a faraway look in her eye.

"You ready for the tour?"

Otis's words brought her back to the present, and Judi nodded, reddening slightly that he'd caught her daydreaming.

"Will this take long? I have to unpack the car, and I need to get groceries, and I really need to rest after the long trip."

"Won't take long at all," he reassured her, "and I put some groceries in the fridge so you shouldn't have to shop for a couple days."

"That was . . . nice of you." Judi wasn't sure she was happy about his thoughtfulness or annoyed that someone she'd never met before had made choices for her.

"So, this room is your mudroom, of course. Agatha used it for her boots when she came in from the garden, and she liked to keep her gardening supplies here too, so they were handy coming in or out of the garden. *Nothing* ever went into the house from the garden except for the vegetables or flowers. None of the fertilizers, seeds, or dirt go into the house."

"Why is that?" Judi said. She looked at Otis in confusion. "Seems like she might have tracked in some of the garden dirt when she walked in, at least."

He opened a door next to the washer and dryer, and there was a small full bathroom.

Judi glanced at Otis and smiled in disbelief. "You are joking, right? I have to shower before going *in* the house? I don't remember ever hearing about my aunt being a neat freak about that type of stuff."

Otis closed the door, pausing before addressing Judi again. "Do *not* bring garden dirt into the house. Believe me, you don't want to. Please take off your shoes out here." He pointed to the large mat to the left of the door where shoes she assumed had belonged to her aunt had been left, as if waiting for her to return.

Deciding to humor her new friend, Judi obediently took off her shoes, and Otis set his next to hers.

They entered the kitchen first. Decorated in her aunt's beloved yellow, the kitchen was large but not *too* large, and outfitted with the newest in appliances. In the center, instead of an island was an old wooden table with four chairs and carved legs containing a pattern of vines and flowers, reflecting her love of gardening. The surprising thing was that there were no live plants in the house. Not one. And for someone who loved her garden as much as her aunt obviously did, Judi found that curious.

She also found curious the design on the carved legs of the furniture. The vines were like nothing she'd seen before. She reached out and traced the pattern with her fingers, marveling at the intricacy of the carving. The vines were thick, the leaves slender with pointed edges like a holly leaf that ended in sharp looking spikes. Strangely enough, they reminded her of fingers spread out as if reaching for something. Very odd. She'd never seen leaves like those before. Small round berries were also spaced out between the vines and the leaves in a grouping of three or five. She was going to have to look this particular plant up to find out the name.

"Ready to move on?" Otis watched her with the same intense scrutiny she'd received from Addie earlier, and once again Judi had the feeling she was being observed. But for what?

Looking further around the house, she again noticed no plants anywhere inside, not even flowers in a vase. Then she realized Otis wasn't joking with his admonition to not bring anything from the garden into the home. Her aunt really did not bring plants inside.

She stood at the kitchen sink and stared out into the garden. The plants were bending slightly in the breeze. She reached to open the window to let in the fresh air, but Otis was at her side in a flash and closed the window almost as soon as she had opened it.

"What?" she asked him in surprise.

He smiled smoothly and motioned her into the next room without explaining his actions, but he remained in place by the window as if guarding it until she left the kitchen to enter the next room.

In short order, they'd gone through the dining room where her aunt's favorite plates were displayed in a pretty arrangement on the wall and also inside a large glass-front cabinet. The plates were adorned with her favorite garden theme, the strange vines and flowers she didn't recognize coiling around them. The cabinet where the plates were stored was carved with a matching pattern to the table in the kitchen, which also matched the table legs in the dining room. The walls were covered in a wallpaper pattern of delicate roses in her aunt's favorite shade of yellow.

The living room contained a large couch, flanked by two small comfortable looking chairs in contrasting shades of gold and a long coffee table, again carved with the same vines. Two narrow tables stood between the chairs and couch, and on each was a crystal statue of vines climbing upward.

Her aunt's fascination with vines was bordering on the right side of obsession, and Judi wondered what that was all about. She wandered about the room while Otis took a call. Her aunt's library held books by popular authors and showed a healthy interest outside the garden as she saw books by mystery, women's lit, and suspense authors. Squinting, she recognized one of the names as a new book she had seen advertised at the local bookstore by the author Sherry Grimes. There were some gardening books in the mix but not too many.

"Ready to go upstairs now?" Otis returned. Leading the way upstairs, he kept up a steady stream of conversation about her aunt's habits, and after a quick look into the three bedrooms and two small bathrooms, both complete with showers and toilet facilities, they returned to the kitchen.

Otis handed her a set of keys from his pocket and explained what each one was for. When he got to the last one, he hesitated.

"This one is for the small shed in the back of the garden, behind the bigger one. But I would advise you to leave that shed alone."

"Why? What's in it?" Judi reached for the keys, which he delayed handing to her for a brief moment, his face thoughtful as he looked at her. She met his gaze and did not lower her eyes.

"There are things that are sometimes best left untouched."

Frowning with confusion, Judi said, "What are you talking about? The shed and the garden and the house are all mine now, right?"

Otis shrugged. "The property is officially yours now," he admitted. "Please let me know if you need anything else."

"Thank you." Judi bounced the keys in her hand for a second before dropping them in her pocket. She walked with Otis to the front of the house and closed the door firmly behind him. She was about to turn away when she remembered the letter he hadn't given her. Opening the door, she was surprised that he was nowhere to be seen, as if he'd vanished in thin air. She would have to find him later and remind him about the letter. With a shrug she returned to the kitchen.

CHAPTER 3

S tanding in the bright room, she smiled. The sun was streaming through the window onto the table. Wanting to let the fresh air inside now that Otis was gone and couldn't reprimand her, she opened the window. Emptying her pockets onto the kitchen table, she hummed as she prepared coffee. Turning back to the table with a steaming cup, she reached for the keys, which were warmed by the sun. They slipped from her hand, and the key Otis had just advised her to forget about disconnected and lay in a sunbeam, which sparked brightly, bringing her attention to it immediately.

Picking up the keys, she put them on the table and reattached the disconnected key. Touching the key, she was surprised to find it warmer than the rest. Looking out the window, she saw the shed shining in the sun as if beckoning her.

"Well, why not?" Grabbing the key, she headed toward the shed.

After unlocking the shed, she stepped inside expecting to find the usual odds and ends of gardening tools or old pots or lawnmowers, along with cobwebs, but instead found it to be clean and dust free. The garden tools were hung carefully on hooks, and a small worktable occupied one half of the wall space to her left. On the right were shelves lined with jars carefully labeled in her aunt's familiar handwriting.

Picking up a few of the jars, she read aloud, "Sunflower seeds, blanket flower, Indian paintbrush, anti-vinum . . . Anti-vinum—what's that?" Her voice trailed off when she picked up the next jar. The seeds in this one were black, thick, and shiny. She opened the jar and poured three of the seeds in her hand, marveling at their substantial weight. They were heavy and bore long black stripes interspersed with deep purple streaks. Stepping outside the shed to get a better look at them, she bounced them in her hand with a puzzled frown. In all her years of gardening, she'd never seen seeds like these.

A warmth spread from the palm in which the seeds rested up her arm to her shoulder.

"Plant me six inches deep, cover me with dirt, and watch me grow."

Judi jumped in surprise. She whirled around at the voice, the seeds flying out of her hand as she turned. Stepping into the soft earth at the side of the shed, she searched for them, but they were gone.

"That was very odd," she thought, peering back into the shed. But as a cool breeze ruffled the ends of her hair, she shivered before turning to lock the shed up and head back to the house.

"Coffee. I think I need more coffee."

A short while later with a fresh cup of coffee in hand, she settled into the chair on the patio as she gazed at her new garden. Everything looked beautiful and vibrant. The flowers were nodding in the breeze that ruffled their leaves every once in a while like the skirts of a dancer, their slender stalks leaning forward then backward.

"What the . . . ?" Judi stood to get a better look. Several stalks of a vine were climbing up the sides of the shed, spreading even as she watched. Bright green leaves with tiny red berries that expanded into cherry-colored fruit grew quickly to the size of tomatoes right before her eyes.

Shaking her head, she scolded herself for an overactive imagination. "Honestly, Judi. Nothing grows that quickly. You are imagining things. It is time for you to get some rest."

She headed inside, closing the door firmly.

An hour later she was snoring softly, vines growing and coming for her populating her dreams. Waking from the nap, she stretched and stared in shock at the living room, which was now covered in green vines that looked remarkably like the carved ones. Their pointed tips reached out as they climbed the wall even as she watched.

Despite being warned to keep the kitchen window closed, she'd left it open to bring fresh air into the stuffy house. The vine had crawled inside the opening.

Not only had the vine crawled inside, but the fruit it bore was splitting open, creating new plants. The black seeds emitted a sickly-sweet odor as if rotting. *Close the window*, was her first thought, but a quick look into the kitchen and she realized that would not be possible as the thick vine had filled the space. Judi's eyes widened as the vine appeared to be pulsing and pushing its way deeper inside as she watched in horror. How could she stop this madness?

"Knife?" she said, but opening the drawer was impossible as the vines had effectively blocked her way to the silverware drawer. She felt a vine tickling her ankle and stepped back, alarmed that the plant was following her. She found a butter knife on the table but hacking at the vine did nothing. The hide was too thick.

"Uh-oh," Judi said, quickly stepping over the vines that were crawling up the walls and across the floors. "I think I need help. But where should I go?"

Immediately the friendly face of the first person who'd talked to her in town, Addie, came to mind. Hurrying from the house and closing the door tightly, she jumped into her car and headed into town. Hopefully, she could find her.

CHAPTER 4

*J*ust as she pulled into the town square area, she caught sight of her new friend. Addie was chatting with some folks but turned when Judi honked.

"Help!" Judi cried out, stumbling from the car without turning the engine off.

Addie hurried over. Taking Judi gently by the arm, she led her to a nearby bench. "What's wrong?"

"I . . . I think something strange is going on at my house . . . No, not 'think'. I *know* something strange is going on."

"Okay." Addie looked at Judi with concern. "Take a breath and tell me what's happened."

Judi quickly explained about the shed, about dropping the seeds, and about leaving the window open and the creeping vines.

"I see." Addie did not look pleased.

"I know I wasn't supposed to go into the shed, but really, I love to garden, and the shed is on my property, and—"

Addie interrupted. "It's okay. We just need to fix this. I'll meet you at the house."

Ten minutes later, the two women were staring at a sight Judi had never thought to see in her lifetime. Tomatoes the size of watermelons were drooping from the house, which was covered everywhere with vines that had broken through windows and were climbing upward like the beanstalk in the childhood stories.

"What . . . has . . . *happened?*" Judi gasped.

"Havenwood Falls has happened," Addie said under her breath. "We need to get some help here. What else was in the shed?"

"Seeds. Jars of seeds . . . Oh, and something called anti-vinum. But I'm not sure what that is."

"It was in the shed?"

"Yes, but the shed is impossible to get into. The vines are completely covering it." Judi was nearly in tears thinking of how she had ruined everything. What an entrance she'd made to a place she'd hoped to call home forever.

"Okay, this is what I need you to do," Addie said. "It's okay. We can fix this."

"I think you ladies might need my help?" Otis Granger spoke up from behind them. "I saw the vines."

"I'm so sorry—" Judi started to say, but Otis cut her apology off with a wave of his hand.

"Enough time for that later. We need to get into the shed before this gets out of control."

"Before this gets out of control?" Judi said with a wry laugh while wringing her hands. "I think it's too late for that."

"Not yet," Otis assured her with a quick squeeze. "Remind me to tell you about the time your aunt . . . Well, time enough for that later, too." Turning to Addie he said, "I have my . . . tools . . . I think I can get the vines near the shed but the rest..."

Addie hesitated and said, "I could just . . . " and she made a gesture with her hands, but Otis shook his head.

"Judi made this mess. How about we let her figure out how to fix it?"

Judi followed this exchange with a confused expression. Something was going on here between the two of them that she was not privy to, and she made a mental note to question Otis about that when this situation was resolved. If it ever could be.

Addie nodded. "Okay. I see your point. I will take care of the rest. You get that anti-vinum. I wish Agatha had listened to me when I asked her to get rid of those damn seeds!"

Addie hurried off in her jeep as Otis and Judi carefully made their way toward the shed. Avoiding the creeping vines wasn't easy, but they made it to the side of the shed with only a few scratches.

The vines here were thick and totally covered the shed, making access to the interior impossible. Judi noted that the vines seemed to stem from a single three-branched root that was near where she thought she'd dropped the seeds.

"Okay, here's what we have to do," Otis said, swatting away a few branches and carefully avoiding touching the fruit. Judi looked at him as a large vine encircled his waist then slid away at the touch of a wand he produced from his pocket.

"What is that?" Judi asked, pointing to the large stick in his hand.

"Yes, well, we can go over that later, too." Otis brushed aside her question. He frowned slightly as he surveyed the scene around them. The vines were slowly turning toward them as if sensing a threat. He waved the stick at them after handing Judi a knife from his pocket.

The sun caught the blade, causing a sharp beam of light to momentarily blind her. She blinked and lifted her hand to shield her eyes.

"When I tell you to," Otis said, "I need you to cut that vine in front of the door with that knife."

"It won't work," Judi said blinking, small dots of light blocking her vision. "I tried already. Nothing cuts their skin."

"This will," Otis assured her. "Ready?"

Judi gripped the knife, nodding at his comment, not really sure he knew what he was talking about. But his confidence increased her belief in him, and she stood ready.

"NOW!" he shouted as another burst of light cut off her vision. Blindly, hoping she was able to hit the right spot, she hacked at the vine, shocked that her blade cut deeply enough that the door was free.

She almost missed her chance, for just as she reached out to grip the door handle, another vine slithered across her wrist, tightening even as she wrenched the door open and fell inside.

Vines tangled around her ankles, causing her to fall with a thud onto the shed's floor, and she felt herself being dragged back toward the door.

"Not today, Satan vines," she yelled as she once again hacked at the branches that were twining up her body with increased urgency. She slipped free of them, stomping on the vines for good measure as they curled up into tight balls then turned to a dark ash.

"Did you find the jar of anti-vinum?" Otis shouted from the other side.

Judi grabbed the jar sitting on the table where she'd left it earlier and turned toward the door. Slipping the bottle into her pocket, she looked up in time to see the vines closing the door from the outside.

She was trapped.

Jiggling the knob and pushing on the door, Judi realized she was truly stuck inside while Otis was outside struggling to free her.

She was on her own. How was she going to get out?

Then a thought occurred to her. If the knife could cut through those thick-skinned vines, perhaps they could cut through the shed. It was worth a try.

Otis was shouting to her from outside, but she couldn't understand what he was saying.

Shouting back, hoping he could hear her, she said, "I'm cutting through the door. Be out there in a jiffy."

She hoped that were true.

She thought about what she needed to do then hacked at the

door. The metal was easy to slice. The knife seemed to know what she was trying to do, and soon she had a small opening cut into the door. The vines also seemed to sense what she had done and were slowly inching their way in even as she worked her way through the small hole. She felt like dogs must when they were going in and out of the doggie door, but she kept wriggling until she was free.

Pulling herself upright, she looked around for Otis, but couldn't see him anywhere in the jungle that had grown up around her, but she could hear him panting as he worked to free her from the other side.

The side of the shed where the original vines had grown was buckling under the weight of the plants that were now at least three layers thick.

"Do you have the anti-vinum?" Otis was out of breath, his hair was wild, and his clothes were in disarray as if he had been in a fight. In his hand the stick was bent, but not broken. He pointed to the side of the shed and said, "Three drops should do it."

Judi looked at him in confusion, not understanding what he meant.

"Three drops of what? Where?"

But Otis was suddenly gone. A vine had grabbed him and yanked him away even as she reached for him.

"Three drops at the root," he shouted before his voice faded into nothing.

Judi glanced down and realized what he meant.

The original vine was shaking, pulsing with life.

Stepping over vines, she made her way to the side of the shed. Bending down, she cleared the dirt from the root and reached for the jar just as a vine snaked its way around her wrist, trapping her hand away from her body. Quickly thinking, she hacked at the vine with the knife, and it broke into ashes. But more were coming.

Seconds. Judi knew she only had seconds. Unscrewing the

top of the jar, she quickly tipped out three drops at the base of the original vine. For a moment nothing happened then the vine shivered and twisted as if in pain. The rest of the vines that had grown from it were on fire, literally, but no heat erupted.

Judi stepped back as the vines began to shrivel and snap back toward their original host. The tomatoes, seeds, and vines all burst into a dark ash. The last to die was the vine on the shed.

A minute later it was over.

The shed was a crumpled mess, the house was definitely going to need some handyman's help, and the yard was filled with a deep layer of dark ash that didn't seem to move with the breeze.

Judi collapsed to the ground and began to cry. She'd made such a mess of her life, such a mess of everything. How could she stay here now? Her aunt's beautiful house and garden were ruined, and it was all her fault.

"You okay?"

She felt the gentle pressure of someone's hand on her shoulder and sobbed louder. How could they be so nice to her after what she'd done?

"I'm so sorry, Otis. I have ruined everything."

"Don't be silly. This was just a little bit of fun. Welcome to Havenwood Falls," he said with a chuckle. He joined her on the ground and pulled her into a side-hug.

"Look at it all." Judi sighed. "I have so much to clean up."

"Not to worry. We can get this fixed in no time. Addie's already getting us help, and in the meantime, you can stay with me. Also, I think I need to apologize to you." He pulled from his pocket the letter he'd shown her before. Was it really so short a time ago? Handing it to her, he said in a voice filled with mystery and worry, "I think this might explain some of this to you. I hope you will understand when you read it just what a magical place you have arrived in.

CHAPTER 5

*J*udi took the envelope and held it carefully in her hands. Turning it over, she read:

Judi,

I hope you find the answers you seek in Havenwood Falls.
Love,
Aunt Aggie

Judi opened the envelope and slipped the letter out. Unfolding it, she settled more comfortably on the ground, liking the permanence and certainty of solid earth under her body, and especially the warmth of a new friend at her side.

The crisp paper crinkled at her touch. Her aunt's handwriting was slanted on the unlined paper and the tiny writing was a little hard to read. Judi squinted and began reading, a smile curving her lips upward at the image of her aunt writing this with all the best intentions.

My dear Judi,

If you're reading this, that means I am gone. I wish we'd had more than a few letters over the years to keep us in touch, but that's life, isn't it? We forget to take the time to do what is important and by the time we remember it's too late.

By now you have met Otis and know that I am leaving you the house, land, and garden that I have been the caretaker for all these years.

I hope you will love it all as much as I have.

I have entrusted my good friend, Otis, to acclimate you to everything. He is dear to me, but a bit . . . unusual. And sometimes, forgetful. Keep an eye on him. I think you two will get along very well.

I hope you receive this letter on your first day here and that you understand what I am about to tell you.

First—Havenwood Falls is a magical place in more ways than one. You will discover its treasures and its secrets as time goes by. Do not hesitate to make friends and reach out to them as needed.

Second—in regards to the garden. It is a miraculous, mysterious, and magical place. There are secrets there as well. Please follow your instincts when it comes to the plants and produce. I know you will understand in time what I mean. Also, as Otis has probably, hopefully, already warned you NEVER bring any of the garden into the house. When you go inside, please remove your shoes first, so you don't track anything inside. If your clothes are dirty, please remember to wash them in the washer just inside the back door, and shower. I know this seems a strange request, but it really is necessary and hard to explain except to say that this is one of Havenwood Falls' secrets, and some secrets should never be challenged or revealed until their time.

I learned a long time ago that I have a responsibility in Havenwood Falls to care for this piece of land. I pass this on to you. I hope you will accept the role I played from the time I arrived until it was my time to go. We are connected to the soil in a unique way. Our talents for gardening will be amplified while living here. Things we grow in this soil will be magnificent—their flavors will be sweeter, the produce will be larger, the flowers will be more aromatic. In Havenwood Falls we possess a magic that isn't all that unusual. Oh, and you will need to get a tattoo. Ask Addie Beaumont or Otis Granger about this. I hope you will stay. Havenwood Falls needs you. My garden needs you.

"You okay?" Otis asked when Judi paused in her reading. His gentle voice was reassuring and calming. Judi turned to the last page of the letter and nodded in answer to his question. She wasn't sure how to take all this information. Magic? She paused before answering.

"She mentions you as a friend I can rely on." Judi smiled shyly at him, lowering her eyes slightly as she turned to glance down at the letter in her lap. "I think she's right. How well do you . . . did you know my aunt?"

"I wouldn't say I knew her well, exactly, but we were neighbors and friends for many years. She had a way with her garden, that's for sure. And she was one of the kindest people I ever knew. You are a lot like her in that regard." Otis turned to look at the mess that was left of the garden. His expression was thoughtful.

"You just met me," Judi said. She was pleased he thought her like her much-admired aunt, but not sure how he could compare them, having only just met her, and in circumstances like these, she had not put her best foot forward that was for sure.

Judi waited, but he didn't say anything else so she returned to the letter.

Third—Otis is a wonderful lawyer and has other talents as well. Take your time getting to know him. I know you'll get along.

Remember, the talent for taking care of the earth runs in our blood. We possess a natural inclination to understand the earth and its secrets, and this garden is evidence of this.

The garden is a very forgiving place. Just take good care of the plants and the house and welcome to Havenwood Falls. I know you will love it as I did.

All my love,

Aunt Aggie

P.S. Don't touch the black seeds. They are pretty, but deadly.
NEVER plant them. If you do, get Addie to help you, or Otis.
They are worse than weeds, and neither must ever enter my
garden. Or, better yet, give them to Addie to destroy.

"Well, I failed that test, didn't I?" Judi muttered to herself, not expecting an answer.

"You didn't fail. I guess you might say the fault is mine." Otis sighed, his sideways glance an apology.

"Why didn't you give me the letter when I first arrived?" Judi was more curious than accusatory as she met Otis's look.

Sighing again, Otis colored slightly. "That was a misjudgment on my account. I apologize. I should have, but . . . " His voice trailed off, and Judi had the instinctive feeling his apology was genuine, but she wasn't ready to let him off the hook that easily. Not after what they'd been through today.

"All this . . . destruction could have been avoided if you'd given me Aunt Aggie's letter."

Otis nodded. Lowering his chin to his chest, he considered his next words. "I knew your aunt had given you this property . . . "

"And you wanted it for yourself?" Judi said. She couldn't think of any other reason than a desire to own this property for his inaction, but he'd never given her a hint that he was interested in her aunt's garden and home. She had a bad habit of jumping to conclusions, and his next words confirmed that she was wrong.

"No. I did not, and do not, want your aunt's home. I liked your aunt very much. She was feisty, funny, and very serious about her garden. She was also very good at creating new plants, thus the seeds for the vine. They came from her cross-pollination of her prize tomatoes and a few unusual Havenwood Falls varieties. But the soil here is . . . different, does things to the plants. You probably already noticed how the flowers are much more aromatic, the vegetables larger and sweeter-tasting, and the herbs more potent. If not, you will see that in time . . . if you stay. To be honest, the reason I didn't give you the letter was because I wasn't sure you would stay, and I didn't want to reveal too much to you before I was sure I could trust you to understand what would be expected of you if you stayed."

He tossed her another of his sideways glances, and Judi colored a little at the intensity of his gaze but didn't answer. She knew what he wanted to know, but she couldn't answer that yet. All of this was so new, and Judi wasn't sure how to take it.

She glanced down at the letter and frowned. Her aunt was right. She was good at science and biology and even herbology and the fact that there was some kind of magic involved was a concept she'd never considered. She stared at her hands, her normal hands. There was nothing magical about them. So where did the magic her aunt mentioned come from?

Was that why she was brought to Havenwood Falls, to continue Aggie's work, to keep her garden alive? Judi glanced around the yard, piles of dark ash and broken furniture a reminder of just how inadequate she was to the task her aunt asked of her.

She had failed, no matter what Otis said to try to reassure her. Her first day here and she'd already destroyed the very garden she was meant to preserve, not to mention the house and the shed.

"I don't know why Aunt Aggie thought this was where I was meant to be." Judi didn't realize she'd spoken the words aloud until Otis answered her.

"Your aunt was a very wise woman. She loved this garden with all her heart. I wasn't kidding when I said I see the same kindness in you as I knew in her."

Judi shook her head, tears filling her eyes. She crushed the letter in her hand and pounded her fists on her thighs in frustration.

"Look at the mess I made of everything." She pointed to the yard as proof of her inadequacy.

Otis laughed. He laughed so hard Judi got angry. Jumping to her feet she shouted, "I made a mess of everything! You can't deny it."

Around her the flowers bent in her direction, their heads bobbing in tune to her anger. She stopped to watch in wonderment as her anger ebbed away, and they settled back to their gentle nodding.

"What just happened?" she said softly, looking around. All the flowers were leaning toward her again as if she was the sun.

"Havenwood Falls likes to test people," Otis said. His tone was serious. "This is your welcome. I think the garden likes you. Trusts you. As do I." He reached for her hand.

Judi looked at the kind man, his face a little dusty with the remains of the ashes of their victory and his eyes so warm. Judi took his hand in hers and smiled at him with reassurance.

"My aunt's letter mentions a tattoo?"

Otis nodded. His smile widened as he caught her meaning. "You will need to get a tattoo. You possess magic, and that is the way those with magic are kept account of. I have a scroll for mine." He rolled up his sleeve to reveal a rolled parchment tattoo with a quill pen next to it.

"I guess a vine would be appropriate, wouldn't it?" Judi said with a chuckle.

The two laughed, and Judi couldn't keep her eyes from his as she realized he gave her hope that more than just a garden would blossom here in Havenwood Falls.

DIMPLES, DISTRACTIONS AND DEAD GIRLS

KRISTIE COOK

CHAPTER 1

$\mathcal{I}$ picked at the blueberry scone that wasn't one-tenth as good as Coffee Haven's, more of it crumbled on the small white plate than ever made it into my mouth. The coffee was even worse, lacking the crispness of being brewed with fresh mountain water—or Willow's magic touch. They were both only props, though, part of my thin disguise as I watched the boy and his father at the table next to the window, skyscrapers looming beyond it and Lake Michigan in the distance. Not that I really needed a disguise, only to blend in.

Finally, they both rose from their seats. The father gathered their trash, and the boy, tall for a nine-year-old, started after him then hurried back to retrieve his nearly forgotten jacket. I stood, too, slowly collecting my things to follow them, but far enough behind that they—or anybody else—wouldn't notice.

I wasn't supposed to be here, not anywhere close to them. There was a small chance I could be putting them in danger, but the bigger threat was if they saw me, if they remembered me, if they remembered our hometown. We'd been warned that the boy, Carter, could become a danger to Havenwood Falls, but more worrisome was that the town, a haven for most, was not at all safe for him. It was best for everyone if he came nowhere near Havenwood Falls again.

Best for everyone but me.

Because sending him away meant sending away the love of my life. Making both of them permanently forget about everything to do with Havenwood Falls, including Addie Beaumont.

My epic love no longer knew I even existed. The only man who'd been able to capture my heart, even with all of his flaws. And there were plenty of those. At least, there had been when he was Atanase "Tase" Roca. Now far away from his family and all of the stigma attached to them, given a fresh start in a new life, he actually seemed to be an even better person than I'd hoped for. If anything, he was a great dad.

The hellhound in me growled softly in appreciation of that. Said hellhound was why I was here in the first place—when she latched onto someone to protect, she wouldn't let go, and she believed Carter was hers to protect. She compelled me to check on him as often as possible, though I'd been holding myself to once a month or so. It was totally my hellhound side's fault that I was here. Totally.

That's what I kept telling myself, anyway.

I followed them out of the coffee shop and onto the crowded sidewalk of downtown Chicago. And promptly lost them. It was a beautiful May Saturday, and it seemed like the whole city was out to enjoy the sunshine, filling the sidewalk and spilling into the streets. Looking to my right, I watched for Tase's dark hair, sure to bob higher than most heads due to his height, but didn't see him. Swiveling my head to the left, I kept my eyes peeled. Still no Tase or Carter.

The intuitive feeling of being watched brushed down my spine. *Fuck. Did he notice me? Did he* recognize *me?* Of course, he would notice me. He was a vampire—his senses were even better than mine. But he should not have recognized me. That spell could not have been broken. If it was . . . *Fuck again.* My back went ramrod straight. How would I explain this? To him, to the Court? I was so screwed.

"Bean." My nickname floated from behind me, said with that voice I missed so much.

Gasping, I reactively spun on my heel. And nearly crashed right into Tase's chest.

His hand darted out for my elbow, catching me before I fell into him. I looked up into his rugged face, his jaw covered in a dark beard, those moroi greenish-gray eyes staring right into mine. The world came to a standstill as our gazes locked. My lungs seized, trapping my breath.

"Tase?" I whispered.

His dark brows knitted together, questions filling his eyes. *Shit*. What the hell was I going to do? My brain knew this was bad, really, really bad. But my heart leapt at the thought that he could never forget me, no matter how sound the spell. Our love was too strong. Our connection too powerful . . .

He gave himself a shake, his eyes clearing and looking at me with . . . nothing. Absolutely nothing.

"Sorry. Didn't mean to run into you," he said, his gaze breaking from mine to find Carter at his side. "Ready to see the Bean?"

I stood there in shock as they hurried off, their conversation about the famous Chicago landmark trailing on the late spring breeze behind them.

Once the moment passed, my heart, only partially healed, shattered all over again. I should have been grateful that he didn't recognize me. That the spell hadn't broken. In fact, I should have known the spell was still intact because part of the magic I'd given him was the ability to be out in the sun, even beyond our town's borders.

Yet the pain felt as fresh as it had the morning he'd left over eight months ago, my heart cracking and splintering all over again, my stomach tying into a knot.

I stood there for another moment, watching them walk

away, trying to release that pain as I also surrendered my attachment to them. Just as I turned to go the other way, something darted out at me and jerked me into the alley, holding me against the wall, a hand over my mouth.

"Are you fucking kidding me, Addie?" the familiar voice growled, moroi eyes glaring at me.

CHAPTER 2

I pulled Michaela's hand off my mouth.

"Dramatic much?" I muttered to my best friend. "What are you doing here? *How* are you even here so fast?"

I just saw her at Whisper Falls Inn this morning, visiting her and feigning a migraine to establish an alibi before sneaking away to create the portal to Chicago. Even with vampire speed, she couldn't have made the 1,300-mile trek in a few short hours. Not even if she'd boarded a plane the moment I left, which was impossible considering the nearest airport was hours from Havenwood Falls.

Without answering, she wrapped her hand around my wrist and tugged me deeper into the alley and the shadows. We stopped at a dead end, and she spun to face me.

Squinting at her, I added, "And what happened to your face?"

"Dragon fire happened to my face," she growled, using her free hand to rub at the blackened skin.

I snorted, trying not to laugh. She was a vampire—she'd heal quickly. "My sweet Princess did that to you?" Then the answers to my own questions dawned on me. "You came through my portal."

"With no help from Leia or the rest of your familiars, thank you very much. Except for the fact that they were guarding the front of our secret cave with a strange ferocity, considering you were nowhere to be found. That's how I figured it out. Now what are *you* doing here?" She shook her head and lifted a hand. "No need to answer that. I know exactly what you're doing, and not only is it not healthy for you, it's downright dangerous for everyone. What happened to making a fresh start, Addie?"

Her greenish-gray eyes were filled with concern as much as the accusation. I shrugged. "He got his fresh start. That's all that matters."

She blew out a harsh breath. "No, you matter, too. We'll have to talk about this at home. Do your witchy-woo-woo thing so we can go before we're missed any more than we already are."

I glanced back down the dark alley, toward the mouth and the sun-drenched street. I could make a run for it. My hellhound side might give me enough speed to at least make it to the crowds before Michaela caught up with me, and she couldn't step into the direct sunlight. Morois didn't immediately burst into flames, but the sun *did* burn them, enough that people would notice smoke rising from her blistering flesh. But what would be the point? I couldn't chase after Tase. I couldn't have a life with him.

I needed to go home to *my* life.

A fresh start would be really nice, but that was awfully hard to do in the town I'd grown up in. I would never leave it, though. It needed me as much as I needed it.

With a sigh, I magically cloaked us so no passers-by would notice, then re-opened the portal. Thirty seconds later, we stepped into the cave in the side of Mt. Sousa, which created the east boundary of the box canyon we called home. Straight below us was the Roca property, which was how we'd found the cave in the first place, when we were kids. We used to hide out here, away from the grown-ups, though we hadn't been back in years. My familiars, aka the beasts—Chewie the silver wolf, Skywalker the black raven, Kylo the tuxedo cat, and Leia the miniature dragon—all greeted me with enthusiasm while giving Michaela dirty looks.

"What made you even look here?" I asked her, swiping the amazonite figure from the center of the protective circle I'd created for the portal and dropping it in my pocket. The stone, carved into the shape of Ganesha, served as my connection to Tase and Carter. As long as I had it, I could find them. Nobody knew that, though. Nobody but Michaela, anyway.

She answered while I worked to release the magic of the circle. "Desperation. I know all of your go-tos, remember? But this was admittedly the last one I thought of."

I could hear said desperation in her voice. "What's going on, Kales? Why did you need to find me so badly?"

"Well, when I realized where you'd probably gone, I needed to make sure you came back! But more importantly, because I lied to your grandmother. To Saundra Beaumont! Do you know how terrifying that is?"

Nodding, I suppressed a smile. My grandmother was as shrewd as she was kind. And you didn't want to be on her bad side. It didn't matter that we were well into adulthood—lying to Saundra Beaumont, or pretty much anyone on the Court besides Michaela, all powerful in their own ways, would make just about anyone feel like a scared kid again.

"I take it she was looking for me?"

"The whole Luna Coven is looking for you!"

Shit. "Why?"

She strode out the mouth of the cave, the beasts and I following her down the mountain. She spoke as we hurried down the overgrown trail that was barely even a path anymore. "The wards were breached. They think, anyway. I guess a few of the witches felt it, but not everyone, so there's confusion. They thought you would know for sure, but you weren't even freaking here. Of course, Saundra figured I'd know where you were."

Double shit. I wasn't only the Court's business manager,

liaison to the Luna Coven, keeper of the town's supernatural registry, and official tattooist, but ever since Yule and Saundra's private confession that she would soon be stepping down from the Court and the High Council of our coven, she'd been dumping more responsibilities on me. Responsibilities such as Chief Warden of the Wards, meaning I was more directly linked to the magical boundaries around our town that protected our secrets and our people.

Stepping up as Saundra's replacement was supposed to be part of my fresh start, which had been difficult to make not only because of my stupid broken heart. Ever since Yule, there had been one thing after another. Just since Spring Equinox, there had been the visit from the Seelie Queen at Willow's baby shower, which required a bunch of memory spells, then the whole fiasco with the Flower Festival and that creep Wyatt. Right after that, Aggie's niece arrived in town and was nearly eaten alive by her own garden and then goddess only knew who else it might have eaten. But even all of this hadn't been enough of a distraction.

"I might have set the wards off when I left," I thought out loud. "Maybe that's why there's confusion." It didn't make complete sense, considering the precautions I took to specifically avoid this, but without more information, I supposed it was a possibility.

"And how are you going to explain that?" Michaela asked, but then she held her hand up, silencing me as she sniffed the air. "Do you smell that?"

I lifted my nose and inhaled, then turned to the northwest, sniffing again. "Blood. A lot of it."

After a shared glance, we took off, sprinting through the forest of aspens and conifers, skirting the vineyards of Stone Falls Winery and hopping Bels Creek, then made our way around the lower part of Mount Alexa on the north side of town. The scent became so strong, I was surprised we beat the Kasun pack or anyone else there. When we stopped, I realized we were in the section of forest right behind my own home.

"Over here," Michaela said, and I hurried over to her as she squatted down to a woman's body partially covered in mud and rotting leaves left from last fall. The mud wasn't created only from the melting snow higher up the mountain but from a pool of blood, still warm. Michaela gently turned the woman over, and we both gasped.

Where her eyes should have been were only gouged out pits.

CHAPTER 3

"*D*efinitely a vampire who did this," Sheriff Ric Kasun declared fifteen minutes later as he examined the body. He turned the victim's arm over to reveal two puncture wounds in her wrist, then pointed out two larger ones in her neck after wiping away a clot of blood and mud. "Possibly two."

He and a few members of his pack had caught the scent, too, arriving on the scene shortly after we had. The others, in their wolf bodies, had left to sniff out any trails while the sheriff shifted into his human form to inspect the scene itself.

"Do you really think a vampire would leave that much blood?" I asked, knowing better.

"Maybe if they were about to get caught," Michaela said offhandedly. Kasun's silvery blue gaze swung to Michaela, full of suspicion. As a wolf shifter, he instinctively hated vampires of all kinds. Realizing her mistake, Michaela hurriedly added, "But why gouge out her eyes? They killed her, so they couldn't be worried about her being a witness against them."

Kasun rose to his full height, dropping his hands on his jean-clad hips, the ends of his flannel shirt bunching over his fists.

"Perhaps to make it more difficult to identify her because there's something special about her eyes. Like moroi eyes . . . "

Michaela crossed her arms over her chest. "What are you implying, Sheriff?"

"I'm *implying* that our victim isn't fully human. I smell something in her blood. Don't you?"

We both sniffed, and I supposed I could smell something faintly different, but Michaela must have picked up on it more. She frowned as her head bobbed.

"Does she look familiar?" Kasun asked her as I squatted down to hold my hand over the drying blood, trying to gauge its magical properties.

"No, but even as rare as we are, I don't pretend to know all of the moroi in the world."

"We're not talking about all of the moroi. We're talking about any who would come to our town." Now Kasun's gaze swung to me. "Like your boyfriend." He practically spat the word.

I suppressed a growl as I stood. "Ex," I reminded him. "And he doesn't remember a thing about our town. Besides, why the hell would he do this? He just happened to attack and kill another moroi, then brought her here—a place he no longer knows exists?"

"Or does he?" The sheriff lifted a brow, and for a moment, I had to wonder if he knew where I'd been, what I'd been doing.

"It doesn't make any sense," Michaela jumped in, distracting him before he scrutinized me any harder. "You know it doesn't. You don't even know if she's a moroi. Can you tell, Addie?"

I shook my head. "Too much contamination. I can't get a good read."

Kasun grunted. "We'll take her to the morgue and get her cleaned up. We'll call you in later, Addie."

Sensing the dismissal, Michaela and I turned toward my house.

"You and the rest of the moroi need to stick around town, too, Michaela," Kasun called after us. "We'll be questioning all of you."

We both spun back around, hands on our hips.

"And all of the other vampires in town, too, right, Sheriff?" I asked pointedly.

"Of course," he muttered.

We turned again and made our way down to my backyard.

"That man just loves to harass us," Michaela complained as we entered my backdoor, the beasts following us inside.

"How can he accuse Tase, though?" I demanded as I banged through my kitchen cabinets. "He hasn't been here for over eight months!" I slammed a cabinet door shut with a groan. "I need a drink. Where the hell is the vodka?"

Michaela tipped her head toward my trash can and the empty bottle on top. "I'm guessing you drank it all?"

"Oh, right. Come on. Let's go to the Knuckle." I already headed for the door.

"It's not even two o'clock," she pointed out.

"So? I need a damn drink!" I glanced over my shoulder at her to see if she was coming.

She remained in place, her brow furrowed with concern. "So now we're day-drinking too?"

I rolled my eyes. "I finished that bottle three days ago. It just finally made it to the trash as I was cleaning yesterday. I'm not becoming an alcoholic, okay? Today's just been . . . too much. Are you coming or not?"

She sighed, following me out the door. "I guess we're day-drinking then."

We grumbled about Kasun as we trekked across town to the Dirty Knuckle, located on the far side of town near the ski resort. Since ski season was over, it was the quieter choice of bars at this time of day.

"We'll have to do some investigating of our own, get him off our backs," Michaela said, placing two mugs of beer on the table in the corner.

"It's not like I can give Tase an alibi," I grumbled as I slid into the booth across from her, "considering I wasn't supposed to see him or even know where he was."

"Speaking of . . . " Michaela said, letting the words hang as a dark brow lifted. When I didn't respond, she leaned closer over the table in front of us, her voice a near whisper. "Why were you there, Addie? What the hell are you thinking?"

Blinking, I averted my gaze, unable to look into her eyes. I shrugged, though I knew she could see right through the false indifference.

"I miss him, Kales," I whispered, swiping at the tear that managed to escape. "I just need to know he's okay. Both of them."

She leaned back in the booth, exhaling slowly. "I know. Xandru does, too." She paused. "You know, Xan misses you, as well. You've been avoiding him, but if anybody knows what you're going through . . . "

I dropped my head into my hands, my drink that I'd wanted so badly completely ignored. Of course, Xan knew what I was going through. This wasn't the first time he'd had to say goodbye to someone he loved. He'd gone through this when Michaela left, too, her memories wiped just like Tase's had been. So had I, though. She was my sister from another mister, and I'd never thought I could feel such a hole in my soul again. Until now.

"You know why I've been avoiding him," I murmured. Although more than a year separated them in age, Xandru looked so much like his older brother that newcomers thought they were twins. It was just hard to see him and not think of Tase. Let alone his and Michaela's too sweet lovey-dovey-ness. They still hadn't passed out of the newlywed stage.

"Well, he still misses you and wants you to know he's there for whatever you need. We're . . . worried about you, Addie." She leaned in again. "I don't want you to become like Xan did when I was gone. You need a distraction, just . . . not in the same way."

Xandru had always been the white sheep in his family of black ones. At least, until he'd lost Michaela, seemingly for good. His distraction had been his father and brothers, all of them involved in some kind of trouble at any given time. I'd done everything I could to keep him and Tase out of the worst of it, but those Rocas had a weirdly tight bond and seemed hellbent on keeping their disreputation.

"Don't get your panties in a bunch over me. I have plenty of healthy distractions." I reminded her of everything Saundra had piled on me as well as all of the "fun" happenings of the past few months.

She cocked her head as I finished, her gaze on the bar on the far side of the room. "Hmm . . . I'm thinking of a different kind of distraction." With a twinkle in her eye and a small smile curving the corners of her lips, she slid out of the booth and stood. "You need to get laid. It's been eight months—don't deny it. Come on. Let's go sit at the bar."

I followed her gaze, then grabbed her arm and jerked her onto the seat next to me. "No! Absolutely not."

"He's hot. And he keeps looking over here. Come on, Bratty Addie, have a little fun."

The stranger at the bar was definitely hot in a way that was almost opposite Tase—light sandy hair, brown eyes, and quite pretty. He looked to be just as tall, though he sat on a barstool, so it was hard to gauge, and if anything, even broader and more muscular than any of the Rocas, which was saying a lot. He appeared to have stepped right out of a magazine, except . . . something told me his looks were deceiving. That he was every bit as bad boy as Tase Roca.

I tugged her closer into the booth, turning her to face me. "I definitely don't need that brand of fun."

She rolled her eyes. "I'm not saying marry the guy. You just need a good fu—" She broke off when I pinched her leg, her bright eyes rounding as she dropped her voice so only I could hear. "He's right behind me, isn't he?"

"Good afternoon, ladies," the sexiest voice I'd ever heard greeted.

CHAPTER 4

"*I* was wondering where the best place to grab a bite would be. The bartender says you two are the ones to talk to. Hoped you might be able to help a visitor out?" He flashed a toothy grin, showing off perfectly straight, white teeth, a dimple popping in each cheek. His gaze lingered a moment on Michaela's left hand, likely noticing the wedding ring, then slid to my face, locking on my eyes.

"Depends," Michaela said, donning her innkeeper, hospitality hat. "What are you in the mood for? Something fancy and romantic for you and your lady or something more casual?"

"Casual," he answered, his warm brown eyes never leaving my face. "No lady for me tonight. Not yet, anyway. Hoping to change that, though." His voice grew less and less sexy with each word he spoke. And then he winked at me. He actually *winked* at me. All because . . . what? I hadn't even said a word to him. What balls! "Maybe . . . pizza?" He continued watching me, apparently asking for my input. Was this his obnoxious way of asking me out? Serious balls. Unfortunately, something fluttered in my belly as those dark eyes twinkled and those dimples deepened.

Shoving it down, I silently lifted a brow. "Pasta? Burgers and fries? Tacos?"

Whoa, I might have given in at tacos, but the Tacos for Daze truck wouldn't be in town today. Thank the goddess. Butterflies or not, this was really not the kind of distraction I needed.

Pushing Michaela out of my way, I slid out of the booth. He grinned wider than before, mistaking my intentions.

"Napoli's is that way, around the corner of the square. Good pasta, great pizza." I pointed in that direction with one hand and then to my left with the other. "Burger Bar is down Main Street that way. Enjoy."

I strode out of the bar as quickly as I could, daring him to follow me.

He didn't, but thankfully Michaela did. I didn't slow my pace as we headed back toward the square.

"That was rude," Michaela said once we fell into step next to each other.

"Right? He was such an arrogant ass."

She snickered. "I meant you."

"Pfft." I waved a hand in the air. "So what?"

She glanced sideways at me. "You're usually so welcoming to newcomers."

"That's my job."

"You do it for more than your job, and you know it. You like people to feel welcome here."

"I like supes to feel welcome . . . if I *want* them to feel welcome. He is human and most certainly doesn't belong here. He'll probably be gone by morning."

"Which makes him a perfect distraction. Your fresh start has to begin somewhere."

"Yeah, well, not there. He may be hot, but I'd end up punching him in the throat just to shut his cocky mouth."

"There are other, more enjoyable ways to shut a man up," Michaela murmured, and I pretended not to hear her . . . or to envision those ways with Dimple Cheeks.

My plans for day-drinking ruined, I left Michaela to check on Xandru and the Rocas to ensure they had alibis for the past twenty-four hours and went home to do a little spell work with the Court's Registry and the town's protective wards. I needed to figure out if a supernatural had, indeed, breached our wards—someone besides me and Michaela. And if it was us, I needed to come up with a reason to give to the Luna Coven and the Court for why we'd suddenly left town without leaving word with anyone.

Once in my sacred space at home, I cast a protective circle, my familiars taking their positions at their respective points. Bringing my needed tools into the center, I dabbed specifically chosen anointing oils on my skin, blended incense herbs and lit them, and placed the crystals and other correspondences around me. Then I settled in the center and dropped into a semi-conscious meditative state.

Within my mind's eye, I sought out the energetic lines that formed a bubble over our town and a twenty-five-mile radius. Envisioning the large, intricate spider web of electric blue light spanning the box canyon and the mountains around it, I followed the lines until I found the break, in a most unusual place. It was just a blip, a small flicker in one of the lines over the forest on Mount Alexa, behind my house—right where we'd found the young woman's body.

The energy attached to the blip definitely belonged to her. Nobody else had entered with her. So she wasn't human, at least a trace of magic in her blood that tripped the wards, but our intruder was no longer a threat, at least. Still, how did she drop in out of nowhere? And was she already dead when she did, or killed as soon as she arrived?

Breaches usually came along the far borders of the wards as supes crossed into our territory on foot, not dropping from the sky almost directly over town, possibly dead or nearly so.

What kind of supe was she? And what the hell happened to her?

As soon as I ended the spell and returned to the physical realm, I hurriedly opened the circle, then rushed out the back door and across my yard. Hopping the fence, I hiked through the forest to the place where we'd found her, at the bottom of where Mount Alexa's slope steepened sharply.

I didn't know what I was looking for, what drove me out here. I supposed I just needed to see the crime scene again without everyone else around. As I inspected the area, spiraling out from where the bloody mud had begun to dry, my witch senses searched for any remnants of energy of something other than the girl. And Michaela. And Sheriff Kasun and his pack. My hellhound senses searched, as well, sniffing and listening for anything dead or alive. There was nothing more than the usual forest inhabitants.

When I came to the clearing that separated this part of the forest from the southeastern edge of Havenwood Heights, the collection of large estates mostly owned by Old Families, I knew I'd gone beyond where that energy blip in the wards would have reached. My eyes scanned the small meadow of wildflowers, the setting sun gilding the fuchsia fireweed, blue columbine, and purple larkspur in golden light, a bright spot in the dark forest.

At the Spring Equinox, I'd led some of the Luna Coven members in a ceremony to plant their seeds of intentions for the coming seasons. We'd written our hopes, wishes, dreams, and needs on homemade paper with seeds pressed into it, then buried them here in this meadow. My intention had been, "I want to just breathe." At the time, it'd been six months since Tase had left, and I'd still felt like I was drowning in sorrow. I'd welcomed in spring with its elemental energy of air, hoping it'd dry up the tears. Apparently, it had dried up my flowers instead. I knew exactly where I'd planted my intentions, on the edge closest to me now—the only ones that were wilted, their heads hanging sadly. I yanked them out of the ground by the root and took them home with me, hoping I might be able to save them, if anything with the tears that still tended to flow.

After feeding the beasts and scrounging up a bite to eat for myself, I delivered my report to the Luna Coven about the woman's bizarre arrival. Text messages flew as we discussed the possibilities, but most of it made little sense because the messages came out of order, thanks to our spotty service here in town. Eventually we gave up and decided to meet tomorrow.

I'd just settled in for the night when Michaela texted me.

> **Kales: Guess who checked into the inn this p.m.? Mr. Dimples McHottie Pants himself**
>
> **Me: You mean McCocky Pants?**
>
> **. . .**
>
> **Kales: I'm sure he has plenty of that in his pants. You need to come over and find out**
>
> **. . .**
>
> **Me: Oh, damn, I already took my bra off. Guess I'm home for the night**
>
> **Kales: You suck. Which one of us is supposed to be the boring old married gal again?**

I bit back the sting of that. If Tase had had his way, we both would have been boring old married gals. But then where I would be now? With him, all memories of my home and life lost?

> **Kales: Sorry. Don't answer that. I guess I'll just let Mammie have her way with Dimples**

I laughed out loud as I envisioned the ghostly form of Michaela's aunt Luiza terrorizing Dimples McCocky Pants with a few butt grabs. That was *almost* worth leaving the house to witness. Almost. Michaela probably knew that would tempt me, but I'd have to disappoint her.

Today's magic had drained me. Tracing the ward lines was easy, but the portals to Chicago and back required a lot of power. If I didn't rest tonight, somebody would notice tomorrow. Somebody as in my grandmother or Sheriff Kasun, neither of whom would be satisfied with anything less than the truth, which they could never know.

Still, as spent as I was, I tossed and turned half the night away and didn't think I'd ever fall asleep. I apparently had at some point, though, because I was in the middle of a dream of Tase watching me make out with Dimples when my phone woke me up.

"Our dead girl is not dead," Sheriff Kasun said before I could even mutter *hello*.

CHAPTER 5

$\mathcal{I}$ couldn't get to the medical center fast enough. It was that time of night that was darkest, the hours just before dawn. The streets were empty and quiet, although there were plenty of residents awake, many running around the forest on four legs hunting their last snack of the night. The medical center itself was lit up brightly, several cars in the small parking lot, including the sheriff's black truck and my grandmother's Lexus. I'd barely stepped foot through the doors of the emergency room when a strong pull in my gut led me straight to the patient's room. Saundra, Mayor Barbie, Elsmed Fairchild, Michaela, and the sheriff spoke with Dr. Underwood in the hallway, but I strode right past them into the private room.

Protect her.

The instinct rushed through me, sending an electric charge down my spine as my hellhound sprang to attention.

The young woman sat up in the bed, her head wrapped in gauze, covering what had once been her eyes. She'd been so concealed by blood and mud in the forest that her features had been indistinguishable, but glossy black hair now curled out from under the white bandages, a mass of tight ringlets nearly touching her shoulders. Her skin was an unnatural mottled gray, but as I watched her drink from the dark bottle in her hands, color returned to her flesh, turning it a beautiful shade of dark sienna. I recognized the label on the bottle. Michaela kept a case of the stuff in her own home at any given time.

"Who's here?" the girl asked, her raspy voice barely more than a whisper and laced with fear. It was hard to tell, but I guessed her to be no more than nineteen or twenty.

I kept my voice low and gentle. "My name is Addie Beaumont. I'm here to help you. What's your name?"

She remained silent for a long moment, and I felt a brush of her energy over mine. *Interesting.* Under the strong vampire charge, it felt like the touch of a witch. She immediately relaxed after reading my energy.

"You're not just a witch either," she said. "There's something else. Wait . . . *hellhound?*" she asked incredulously. "But . . . why do I feel so safe with you?"

I took this as my cue to move farther into the room, closer to the bed. "You *are* safe with me. Hellhounds are very protective of those who need it. Do you want to tell me your name?"

The bandages across her eyes moved, as though her brows scrunched together. I felt her push against my energy again, and I must have passed her test. "Niquinya but please call me Quin."

"It's nice to meet you, Quin. So you're a witch too?"

Her bottom lip disappeared between her teeth, her chin trembling as she gave a barely perceptible nod of her head. "*Was* a witch," she said, "until . . . "

She fell silent, and a moment later a bloody tear leaked from under the bandages over her eyes and rolled down her cheek.

Moving right up to her bed, I gently touched her forearm, grateful when she didn't flinch. Rather, she relaxed even more.

"Until what? What happened, Quin?" I whispered.

"I . . . I don't remember."

"What's the last thing you do remember?"

She inhaled a shuddering breath and slowly released it before setting her bottle on the table that stretched across the bed. She did it so easily that it was hard to believe she was blind. The heightened vampire abilities combined with her witch senses would serve her well. She was still a witch—that I was most certain of now that I could get a good read on her.

"Um . . . I was, well, on a *job*—" The way she said the word made it sound like it was not normal work, but I didn't want to interrupt her with questions now that she was finally talking. "—and I saw my chance for escape, so I ran. I ran as fast and as hard as I could. The farther I got away, the more I felt my magic returning, but then . . . " She shook her head. "I don't know. I was trapped. I couldn't move. And the next thing I knew, I woke up freezing cold and screaming, unable to see, and my throat burning with the need for blood. They said . . . they said I was in the morgue. That I freaking *died!* I can't . . . I can't believe this happened."

"You don't remember who turned you?"

She shook her head. "I don't remember any of it. Just running and then paralyzed."

"Why were you running?"

Her voice hardened now. "From traffickers."

"Traffickers?" I asked, a sick feeling settling in my gut.

"Six years ago, I was taken from my coven in Maryland. Snatched by these magic traffickers led by a demon in Northern California. They dragged me across the country and had me do . . . awful, awful things. The kinds of things that make the humans fear witchcraft, calling it the devil's work. It literally was." A shudder wracked through her body. "They kept my magic suppressed unless I was on a . . . a job, as they called it. That last time, when I ran, I was supposed to be working a spell to entice another young witch away from her coven. I couldn't do it, though. I couldn't bring another soul into that terrible life. They squashed my magic when I refused, but then . . . it was like a miracle. My chance to escape." She hiccuped. "I almost made it. I was *so* close."

Another bloody tear rolled down her cheek.

"You couldn't be in a safer place," I assured her, gently squeezing her arm. "Did they tell you where you are?"

She shook her head again. "I just know I'm in a hospital, and there are a shit-ton of supernaturals around here. I can sense so many."

"Your witch powers are still strong."

"That's weird, right? I can't believe I'm a vampire. I don't want to hurt any more people!" Panic ripped through her voice.

"Shh . . . it's okay. Breathe through it. Just breathe." I gave her another reassuring squeeze, not letting go until she nodded. "You don't have to hurt anyone. We can help you. You're in a place called Havenwood Falls. It's a safe haven for people like us. Like you." I proceeded to tell her all about our town. "If it's what you want, you just might find that this is the perfect place for you to have a fresh start at your new life. You can stay with me, to start with. If you want."

The words tumbled out of my mouth before I knew what I was even saying.

I'd become known as a sort of big sister to many of our town's young supernatural girls who'd stumbled into our canyon with powers they didn't know they had. They were always freaked out, even more than Quin was, and I had a way of helping them through acceptance and then embracing their abilities. One of my favorite things was watching young women become empowered as their true, authentic selves. When I discovered my hellhound side, I came to realize that this was part of her protective nature. Still, I wasn't usually *this* welcoming. To invite a stranger into my *home*? My hellhound was taking this one seriously. Perhaps she suspected Quin wasn't out of danger yet.

The sheriff wasn't keen on the idea of releasing her to me, but Dr. Underwood said there was no reason to keep her in the hospital. He gave her the all-clear, confirming that the transition had healed her injuries, although it couldn't remake her eyeballs. Unfortunately, no magic could do that.

"Who better to watch over her than Adelaide?" Saundra asked Ric as we stood out in the corridor. "You can't hold the girl. She hasn't broken any law."

"That we know of," the sheriff replied, rubbing his jaw as he eyed *me* suspiciously. Which girl was he referring to anyway? Or did he already know what I'd done yesterday? "Her arrival is certainly irregular."

"So like Saundra said, who better to watch over her than Addie?" Michaela said. "She's the keeper of the wards, does the tattoos, and is probably one of our town's fiercest protectors. Sindi and I will help her with the vampire stuff."

"The last place she should be is at the inn," Ric nearly growled.

"Exactly," Michaela agreed. "We are pretty full with guests anyway."

"I'm not going anywhere except with Addie," Quin called from her room. "If my input matters at all. I trust her."

"We all do," Mayor Barbie said pointedly.

"Fine," the sheriff finally conceded. "If anything happens, I'm holding you accountable. If anyone goes *missing*, even if just for a few hours, I'll be knocking on your door."

Shit. Was that an innuendo? I couldn't fathom how he could possibly know about my trip out of town—"just for a few hours"—when Saundra didn't even seem suspicious, but it was the only thing that could explain his attitude toward me. He didn't really have a beef with me, per se. It was who I hung out with, the vampires, that rubbed his fur the wrong way. More specifically, the morois. He'd never understand why I'd risk everything for one of them. Truthfully, I couldn't blame him.

For the sake of all of us, I had to stop visiting Tase. Otherwise, sending him away was pointless.

CHAPTER 6

*A*fter giving Quin her new tattoo that not only linked her to our wards but would allow her to walk in the sun, I took her home, describing everything for her as I went.

"I hope you don't mind my familiars," I said as we climbed out of the jeep in my driveway. "They're a little . . . uncommon."

She laughed when she met the beasts, the first time I'd heard her do so, and she was in awe with Princess Leia.

"You have a lot of potted plants, don't you?" Quin said, holding onto my elbow as we entered the front door once the beasts allowed us in. Her head moved left to right, as though she was looking around. "An impressive collection of herbs." She sniffed. "Is that self-heal?"

"Wow. Impressive." It wasn't a common herb, especially not to keep as a potted plant, but its medicinal qualities were unequaled, so I kept it on hand. Unlike other members of the mint family, its scent was so subtle that only a vampire could smell it and only a witch would know it. If she could learn to accept her new existence and make the most of it, Quin could do extraordinary things with this combo of powers.

She released my elbow, easily making her way through the small living room and into the kitchen, where yesterday's wildflowers looked even worse now, drooping in their vase on the table. I should probably just throw them out. "Thought I smelled flowers, too."

"Are you an elemental witch?" I asked, catching on.

"Earth has always been my favored element. When I was little, my nana . . . " Her voice trailed off, and I assumed she was lost in the memory, but when she spoke again, I realized she was overcome with emotion, her voice thick with tears. "I'll never see her again. I'd always had this tiny bit of hope, but now . . . she can't see me like this."

I frowned. Surely her own grandmother would still love her, regardless of her new dietary preferences. However, I wasn't familiar enough with the girl to presume anything about her coven or her family dynamics, and until we figured out the full story of how she came to Havenwood Falls, it was probably best she didn't think about going home right now. She was likely still being hunted. Havenwood Falls and I could protect her when nobody else could or would.

Michaela must have stopped by while I was doing Quin's tattoo, because a case of blood bottles from Stone Falls Winery was already in my fridge. From what I understood, the bloodthirst was the worst in the first few months, so I handed Quin a fresh bottle before showing her to the guest room and then the bathroom we'd be sharing. Unsurprisingly, she acclimated to her surroundings quickly.

After we both showered and dressed, I gave her a pair of dark shades to cover her sutured eyelids, then took her out to get a new phone and stop by Callie's Consignments for some clothes. She had more curves than I did, so my clothes were a little too snug on her. Michaela and Sindi met us back at my place in the afternoon to give her vampire lessons while I met with the Luna Coven.

"Whoa," I said as I dropped into the kitchen chair later that evening. We'd had pizza with Michaela and Sindi, then they had to go, Michaela to see Xandru and Sindi to work the night shift at the inn. After seeing them off, Chewie and I did a quick perimeter check, just to be sure. There had been no more blips in the wards, but the coven was still just as confused with Quin's appearance as we were yesterday. I couldn't be too careful with my new charge. "Did you seriously just grow that?"

Quin smiled sheepishly from the other chair, a small clay pot between her hands with a new green shoot uncurling as I watched. I recognized the pot from a stack next to my sink that I'd cleaned the other day, after transplanting their contents into the ground outside.

"I hope you don't mind. Your wildflowers needed some new life, so I took some of their essence and made . . . new life."

At a loss for words, my mouth opened and closed, and if I hadn't been the one to take and test her blood for the Registry, I would have wondered if she had something besides witch in her DNA. This power reminded me of the new moon fae in town, but it tasted different, so certainly not fae. Definitely elemental magic, like my fire magic, but with the cool, umami flavor of fresh earth.

"It makes me feel more normal," she continued. "More like myself, even with this constant burn in my throat. Sindi promised it would eventually subside, and at least here in Havenwood Falls, I could live almost as normally as possible. But normal to me is this." Her finger easily found and caressed the growing leaf. "I'm so grateful I can still do this. It gives me . . ."

"Hope," I finished for her when it seemed she couldn't say the word herself.

She nodded. "Hope," she echoed tentatively, as though testing the word on her tongue. "Hope for a new life. A fresh start. That's all I wanted, really."

"You and me both, Quin," I said. "This can be a fresh start for both of us."

"How for you?"

I stood. "That story requires some booze. Good thing I replenished the coffers today."

Pulling two glasses out of the cabinet, I retrieved a bottle of Stone Falls extra-special mix of blood and wine for Quin and filled my glass from the box of chardonnay in the fridge. As I poured her glass, I began to tell the short version of my story with Tase. She didn't need all the gory details, and she especially didn't need to know the real reason I'd let him leave—that I'd sent him away.

"To new beginnings," Quin said when I was done, lifting her glass.

I clinked mine against hers while watching the Colorado columbine she'd grown bloom. "And for seeing how we blossom from here."

I awoke with a start, and it took me a moment to realize Quin had wakened me. Her gasps had, actually. Jumping out of bed, I darted out of my room and across the hall. She sat up in bed, gulping for air.

"A dream?" I asked, sitting on the bed next to her.

She shook her head. "No. I couldn't sleep. I remembered something."

"What?" I demanded, probably a little too harshly.

"The last face I remember seeing before I was knocked out or killed or whatever. A white man. Tall and muscular. Light brown hair and dark brown eyes."

My hellhound growled. "Let me guess—a pretty face with dimples for days?"

She inhaled sharply. "How do you know?"

"Stay. Put!" I nearly shouted as I sprang out of her room and back to my own, grabbing my phone and dialing the inn as fast as I possibly could. Sindi picked up. "Watch Dimples' room and don't let him leave! Call Michaela and tell her to meet me there. We have a problem!"

"Um . . . okay. But—"

I didn't wait for her buts, disconnecting the call so I could pull a hoodie on and shove my feet into the first shoes I found.

"Chewie and Leia, guard Quin," I ordered before hurrying out of the house. He shouldn't have been able to break through the wards on my house, but he must have somehow broke through the town's protection—and fooled both Michaela and me. I *swore* he was human. What was he that he could hide so well?

I'd hadn't even backed into the street yet when there was a pounding on the jeep's window, making me jump.

"He's not at the inn," Michaela said from right outside the passenger side.

"We need to call—"

Michaela's hand shot up, silencing me as she cocked her head. Then she tipped it toward the back of my house.

Shit. He was already here.

Leaving the jeep running to hopefully hide any noise we made, I slid out, and we each took a different side of the house to circle around. He wasn't on my property, though. He was just behind it, barely inside the forest's edge. I stopped under the cover of my greenhouse to watch him, signaling to Michaela, who crouched on the far side of the shed. He didn't seem to see either of us, or sense us in any way. Whatever kind of supe he was, his senses sucked, which was good for us. Or maybe he was just really good at hiding any reaction.

Close enough to be able to do so, I tugged on the magical connection to my familiars. Chewie and Skywalker flew out of the house, and that was the first reaction Dimples gave, jumping at the sight of the wolf, then scrambling backward into the forest as Chewie ran then sprang over the back fence, Skywalker flying next to the large wolf. Michaela and I took advantage of the opportunity and charged.

She beat me to him, but the man swung out at Chewie's lunging fangs and large paws, missing the wolf but pummeling my best friend in the shoulder, sending her back several paces. I sent a spell at him, magically binding him at the same time Chewie's paws hit his shoulders, knocking the oversized asshole to the ground. Slobber hung from the wolf's large fangs as he growled right in Dimples' face.

But Dimples wasn't so easily frightened. Maybe everything *had* been a ruse, and he had more abilities than I'd given him credit for. Because the next thing I knew, he head-butted my familiar in the snout, hard enough to make Chewie cry out and flinch back. Dimples writhed against my bindings, although in vain, unable to break through them. Chewie's mouth opened wide, a snarl deep in his throat, and he was about to attack when Dimples' head suddenly bounced sideways with a loud clank and his whole body went limp.

"Asshole," Michaela huffed, tossing the shovel on the ground. A trickle of blood flowed into the dirt under said asshole's head, not all that far away from where we'd found Quin in a much larger pool of crimson mud. Served him right for whatever he'd done to her. Michaela crouched by his head, checking his eyes to ensure he was really unconscious while I dropped to my knees next to him then rolled him to his side, fishing his wallet out of his back pocket.

I threw it at her. "Check his IDs, Kales. I bet he gave you a phony name at check-in."

While she did that, I patted him down, finding a gun in a holster under his shirt. "What the hell?"

"Oh, shit," Michaela whispered at the same time. She thrust something at me. "We just knocked out a Fed."

"*What?*" I studied the badge she waved in my face, then my breath left me, my whole body feeling as limp as the one on the ground in front of us. This was bad. So fucking bad.

Michaela spoke the words that were caught in my throat. "Why is the FBI in Havenwood Falls?"

. . .

To be continued . . .

Stay up to date about our next anthology, coming in Summer 2022, catch up on the dozens of Havenwood Falls titles, and discover more at www.HavenwoodFalls.com

Subscribe to our reader group and receive free stories and more!